VLORs & VICE

VLORs & VICE

The Unveiling of Agents Z and Rahz

Book 1

S E A N L J O H N S O N

VLORS & VICE
THE UNVEILING OF AGENTS Z AND RAHZ

iUniverse books may be ordered through booksellers or by contacting:

iUniverse
1663 Liberty Drive
Bloomington, IN 47403
www.iuniverse.com
1-800-Authors (1-800-288-4677)

Because of the dynamic nature of the Internet, any web addresses or links contained in this book may have changed since publication and may no longer be valid. The views expressed in this work are solely those of the author and do not necessarily reflect the views of the publisher, and the publisher hereby disclaims any responsibility for them.

ISBN: 978-1-4917-8002-2 (sc)
ISBN: 978-1-4917-8001-5 (e)

Library of Congress Control Number: 2015917038

Print information available on the last page.

iUniverse rev. date: 10/20/2015

Synopsis

In a modernized, futuristic society, the year 2107, everything is at peace. All wars have been eliminated from the world, thanks to a secret agency no one has ever seen before. Murder rates are at the lowest they've been in almost fifty years. However, because of how many Americans (and other citizens from around the world) feel about the US government, there will always be some kind of anarchy.

The story begins in Hidendale Springs, Illinois, where one lucky young boy ...and one girl will go on the ride of their lives—a journey they never would've imagined and one that includes learning who they really are inside.

Season 1, Episode 1

Monday, April 10, 2107

Darkness fills the surrounding area. A young boy opens his eyes. He notices that he is floating among the stars in outer space. He is wearing a full-body space suit and drifting toward an unoccupied star cruiser. The boy reaches the star cruiser and straps himself into the pilot's seat in the cockpit. The star cruiser will aid him as he gets ready to pilot the cruiser in an intergalactic space battle against enemy creatures from other worlds.

ZADARION. All right, let's get this show shifted to full speed. *He puts on a radio headset and presses the call button, calling Command Base Center.* Pilot Z to Command Base Center. Do you copy?

COMMAND BASE CENTER. Read you loud and clear, Pilot Z. Prepare to get in formation with the other star cruisers. The battle is about to begin.

ZADARION. Copy that! *He ends the call and then drives his star cruiser in line with the rest of the cruisers.*

PILOT ACE. Ah, Pilot Z. Where you been, man?

PILOT F-BOMB. Yo, you was about to miss all the action.

ZADARION. I'm sooo glad that I made it here just in time then. *He revs his ships engine.* But now, let's kick some serious space booty.

The battle begins. Pilot Z and Pilot Ace, along with Pilot Zenara and Pilot F-Bomb, fly in different directions to avoid central fire. There are several star fleets to destroy, and Pilot Ace and Pilot F-Bomb are targeting those ships, while Pilot Z and Pilot Zenara head straight toward the main battle cruiser. Pilot Zenara gets hit by two shots from different aerial cruisers and loses her reflector shields. Pilot Z swoops down to protect Pilot Zenara's star cruiser, and he blasts three enemy cruisers into oblivion.

PILOT ZENARA. Thanks, Pilot Z. *Sees four cruisers aiming at Pilot Z and shouts.* Wait! Look out behind you, Z! *Shoots down the four cruisers that were heading toward Pilot Z.*

ZADARION. Thanks, pretty girl. *Winks while his ship flies past Pilot Zenara's.*

The battle is looking promising for the four young heroes. The enemy cruisers are now reduced to one main battle cruiser and three smaller cruisers. Pilot Z and Pilot Zenara fly straight toward the main battle cruiser, with Pilot Ace and Pilot F-Bomb following behind them. Suddenly, an identical enemy star cruiser emerges from the dark and blasts Pilot Zenara's star cruiser into pieces. Pilots Ace, Z, and F-Bomb become furious. Pilot F-Bomb targets the newcomer with open fire, but it is only 67 percent effective. Pilot F-Bomb is targeted next by one of the smaller cruisers, but Pilot Ace swoops in and delivers a nonstop assault. Pilot Z instructs the others to distract those cruisers long enough so he can get a clean shot. But the main battle cruiser sneaks behind Pilots Ace and F-Bomb and blasts their ships to pieces. Surprisingly, Pilot Ace's damaged ship comes out of the explosion, shoots straight at the three leftover enemy cruisers, and self-destructs. Pilot Z angrily flies toward the enemy star cruisers and …

DAVE MIKAELSON. *He flicks Zadarion's right ear, waking him from his dream.* Wakey, wakey for eggs and bacon. *Laughs.*

ZADARION. *He starts rubbing his throbbing ear.* Ow. *He blinks and shakes the dream from his head as he looks around the classroom.*

MITCH CONALD. *He starts mimicking Zadarion but in a girlie voice.* Ow. Heh-heh.

PROFESSOR COLUSSON. *He turns his body around from the dry-erase board to face the entire class and clearing his throat.* Ahem. Am I bothering you, Mr. David?

DAVE MIKAELSON. *He is looking annoyed.* No. And it's Dave.

PROFESSOR COLUSSON. Well, Mr. Dave, will you and your posse consider not interrupting my lesson. I'll assume you wouldn't want your so-called friends to experience a Granny Mikaelson teaching lesson, am I right?

DAVE MIKAELSON. *He sits up straight in his seat and facing the dry-erase board.* Yeah whatever. My bad.

RICH DAVIS BLOOME. *He is snickering and whispering so only Dave can hear him.* Soft as ever.

DAVE MIKAELSON. *He's sneering and then looking at Zadarion.* After class, prick.

ZADARION. *He gulps and focuses his attention on the clock in front of him.*

At Centransdale High School, the school bell rings, and students flood the halls, heading to their lockers.

Centransdale High School is two different buildings that are connected via glass tunnels. These tunnels are accessible from the outside and through the hallways. Centransdale is kindergarten through the twelfth grade.

All the students are gathering their belongings, conversing with one another, and exiting the premises in a timely manner. Zadarion is among the first few to exit the school. He heads down the street and turns the corner onto Westick Blvd., only to be seen by Dave, Mitch, and Rich. These are the school's "cool kids," who love to torment and bully smaller kids. Zadarion frantically tries to run, but Mitch grabs his arm. Rich walks up to Zadarion and puts his arm around his neck in a friendly manner.

RICH DAVIS BLOOME. Come on. Walk with us, Zadarion. *Grins like he's up to something.*

The three young boys are sixteen years old. Rich Davis Bloome is a somewhat spoiled brat, who loves attention, likely because he doesn't get it at home. His parents are wealthy individuals who work all the time in order to provide for their son. Mitch Conald is a middle class suburban kid who grew up in HighTech City, Georgia. He is a follower. Without his two companions, Mitch would never bully anyone. Dave Mikaelson lost his mother at a very young age and acts out by inflicting harm on others. Dave's grandmother, on his father's side, is not someone you would want to mess with. Dave's grandmother is not aware what Dave is like at school. Dave has a knack for talking himself out of trouble.

The three young boys walk Zadarion to an alley, near a donut shop, where they plan to beat him up.

MITCH CONALD. *He's pushing Zadarion to the brick wall.* Now, daydream your way out of that.

RICH DAVIS BLOOME. *He is pulling Mitch away from Zadarion.* Nah, bro, this is Dave's problem. *Nods to Dave.*

DAVE MIKAELSON. *He's cracking his knuckles while walking toward Zadarion.* You want this to hurt?

ZADARION. *He's flinching and speaking in a trembling tone.* No.

DAVE MIKAELSON. *He punches Zadarion in his stomach and knocks him to the ground.* Make me look like the bad guy in class now, huh?

MITCH CONALD. Ooohhh, that gotta hurt. *Laughs.*

DAVE MIKAELSON. Get up! *Pulls Zadarion up by his shirt collar and pushes him to the brick building.* Did you just frown at me? *Punches Zadarion again, this time in his chest.*

ZADARION. *He is breathing in and out slowly, to calm himself.* Please. I didn't do anything! Leave me alone.

DAVE MIKAELSON. *He grabs Zadarion's shirt collar and gets ready to punch him in the face.*

RICH DAVIS BLOOME. *He grabs Dave's arm.*

DAVE MIKAELSON. Dude?

RICH DAVIS BLOOME. *He points to a man standing in front of the alley's entrance.*

CONVENIENCE STORE CLERK. Hey, let the kid go, you punks! *Walks closer to them.*

RICH DAVIS BLOOME. *He's putting his hands out.* Heyyyy, there's no need. We out anyway.

DAVE MIKAELSON, *letting go of Zadarion's shirt collar and whispering to him.* You lucky, prick. *Pushes Zadarion on the ground and walks away.*

Dave, Rich, and Mitch walk away from Zadarion, passing the convenience store clerk and leaving the alley. The convenience store clerk helps Zadarion get up off the ground.

CONVENIENT STORE CLERK. Well, you look all right. That's good. You need to tell someone, kid. Don't be ashamed to snitch on those punks. *Walks back to his store.*

Zadarion looks at the ground for a minute and then wipes his face. Zadarion runs home. Before entering his home, Zadarion makes it look like he was not attacked. He takes a cloth out of his book bag, wipes his face clean, and puts the cloth back into his bag. Zadarion walks in the house and smells something sweet being prepared in the kitchen.

ZADARION. *Sniffing.* Mmm, that smells great. Mom, what smells so good?

MRS. HAILIE JONES. Well, welcome home, sweetie. *Walks to her son, kisses her son's forehead, and continues preparing the meal to be eaten at dinnertime.* My special dessert for *after* dinner, absolutely no asking early.

ZADARION. *Walking over to his baby sister, Kiley, and makes funny faces at her.*

KILEY. *She laughs, as she always does when he does this.*

ZADARION. All right, Mom. Hey, has Dad been here today?

MRS. HAILIE JONES. He stopped by around eleven in the afternoon.

ZADARION. What about Grandpa?

MRS. HAILIE Jones. No. But he should be at home right now. You going to visit him?

ZADARION. Oh yeah.

MRS. HAILIE JONES. All right. Have fun, sweetie.

ZADARION. Later, Mom. *Rushes out the door.*

Zadarion runs as fast as he can to his grandfather's place, only to be intercepted by his best friend, Sam Kerry. Sam Kerry is Zadarion's only friend. The two met when they were five years old.

SAM KERRY. Going to visit your grandfather again, aren't you, Zada?

ZADARION. *Chuckling.* You already know.

SAM KERRY. Guess it is that time of the month. *Laughs.*

ZADARION. Ohhh. So not called for. *Laughs along with Sam.* You're a funny dude. *Stops laughing.*

SAM KERRY. *Stops laughing too, realizing his friend has stopped.* They messed with you again, didn't they?

ZADARION. *Nodding.* What about you?

SAM KERRY. They beat me up yesterday. I stayed after school today playing chess until my mom picked me up. They weren't going to get me again. *Sighs.* We can't keep this up forever, brother.

ZADARION. Yeah, I agree. *Sighs.* So, where are you off to?

SAM KERRY. Just going to the grocery store for my mother, then my dad's coming to visit. He's taking me golfing!

ZADARION. That's awesome. But on Saturday, you and I are still on for the movies, right?

SAM KERRY. Oh heck yeah! I wouldn't miss it, brother.

The two friends shake hands and depart. Zadarion walks to his grandfather's house. When he arrives, he rings the doorbell. He rings it several times, and no one answers. This is strange to Zadarion.

ZADARION. Come on, Grandpa, answer the door. *Realizes he has the keys to his grandfather's place and reaches into his pocket for the key. Opens the door and sees that the lights are turned off.* Hellooooo? Grandpa. Are you there?

There is not a sound in the house. Zadarion searches each room and decides to leave.

ZADARION. *Mutters to himself.* He must be at the market. Maybe I can meet up with him there. *Leaves.*

While on his way to Cuues Marketplace, on Venue Ave, Zadarion sees Dave Mikaelson talking with an older female and decides to take the long way. Luckily, Dave didn't see Zadarion. While walking with his hands in his pockets, Zadarion looks up. Twenty feet ahead of him, three individuals dressed in black suits are pulling something or someone (it's hard to tell) into an alley. Zadarion passes the alley, and he could swear he just seen his grandfather's head vanish into thin air. Doing a double take, Zadarion walks backward and stares into the empty alley.

ZADARION. What the—? *Stands frozen in place.*

POLICEMAN. *Walking by Zadarion.* Lose something, kid?

ZADARION. *Snapping back to reality.* What? No! I-I gotta go! *Runs back toward his grandfather's house, the puzzled look on his face making it clear he's not sure he can believe his eyes. He says out loud to himself.* That could not have been you. Could it?

Zadarion makes it to his grandfather's place. This time, without knocking on the door, he unlocks it and forces his way inside the house. He bumps into his grandfather.

GRANDPA JEDEDIAH JONES. Whoooaaaa. *Catches himself from falling using his cane.* Where's the fire?

ZADARION. *Grandpa!* I just— I thought—

GRANDPA JEDEDIAH JONES. Breathe, son.

ZADARION. *Taking a deep breath and exhaling.* Why weren't you here earlier? Were you at Cuues Marketplace?

GRANDPA JEDEDIAH JONES. I was out back taking out the trash.

ZADARION. *Remembering that the trash is in the front of his grandpa's house.* You were out back taking out the what?

GRANDPA JEDEDIAH JONES. *Coughing loudly.* Oh, excuse me. My old age. *Laughs.* I mean, I was out back in my pantry.

ZADARION. Oh. I should've checked there. *Shrugs off his suspicions.* So, guess what, Grandpa?

GRANDPA JEDEDIAH JONES. Oh please do tell, my oh-so-favorite grandson.

ZADARION. What? *Becomes confused but again shrugs it off.* Well, today at school, my English paper won first place. I got a scholarship, and with it, I get to go on a trip to Hidendale Observatory. I get to see that new exhibit with all twenty planets! Isn't that exciting?

GRANDPA JEDEDIAH JONES. *Smiling.* My grandson the genius. *Hugs his grandson.*

ZADARION. I told you first. When Mom finds out she's gonna freak out! *Laughs and then stops.* Oh, wait? *Checks the time.* I gotta go. Bye, Grandpa.

Grandpa Jedediah Jones's smile fades from his face after Zadarion walks out the door. Soon after that, Grandpa Jones drops the cane on the floor, steps over it, and walks to the kitchen.

ZADARION. *Reenters the house. Seeing his grandfather's cane on the floor, he becomes worried. He picks up the cane. He hears noises coming from the kitchen and goes to check it out.* Grandpa?

GRANDPA JEDEDIAH JONES. *Collapsing on a nearby chair.* Oh. I thought you had left.

ZADARION. I forgot to say good night. *Hands his grandfather his cane.* Are you sure you're all right?

GRANDPA JEDEDIAH JONES. Positive. You run along home now. Don't want your mother to get all worried.

ZADARION. Right. Good night, Grandpa. *Leaves the house. Ponders the situation, muttering to himself as he walks home.* His oh-so-favorite grandson? Pfft. I'm his only grandson. *Shakes his head.* Whatever, I'm hungry as ever. *Laughs.*

Arriving at his house, Zadarion cleans up and heads down for dinner. Another night without his father at the dinner table is pretty normal. Suddenly, Kiley Jones made a mess of her dessert. She threw her dessert on the kitchen walls and on the floor then she started laughing. Zadarion starts laughing and forgets about his father not being present. Mrs. Hailie Jones is not pleased. She did not yell at Kiley but she is pissed that she has to clean the kitchen again and give Kiley another bath. Zadarion went to bed and slept well that night.

Tuesday, April 11, 2107

The next morning, Zadarion gets dressed for school. He grabs his school gear, dashes down the stairs, grabs a snack, and speeds out the door after saying, "Later, Mom." While walking to school, he runs into Sam Kerry, and the two walked to school together. The school day drags on and on, the day is completely dry—in other words, boring.

After a long and boring day at school, Zadarion is glad to hear the bell ring. He hesitates for a minute before leaving the premises because Dave Mikaelson is waiting for him outside of the school, on Westick Blvd. Zadarion goes back through the schools doors, exits through one of the side doors and runs, making his way to Blake Street and running across the street. There's an NH Pharmacy on that street. He's obviously taking another way home to avoid Dave. He's walking down Florestse Street, passing many stores, when he notices Dave's friends Rich and Mitch. Zadarion knows Dave must be nearby, so he decides to turn around and continues down Valmar Street. After ten minutes, the trio is somewhere else, Zadarion lost them. Zadarion is too busy looking over his shoulder to see if Dave and his buddies are still behind him. Zadarion is not paying attention to what's on the ground and he trips over an object, falling forward and scraping his right knee on the concrete.

ZADARION. *Sitting on the ground holding his knee.* Ow.

Zadarion looks around him to determine what tripped him, but he sees nothing. He suddenly feels a slight pinch on his upper right arm. He scratches the spot on his sleeve and stands up but does not check his arm. Zadarion starts walking home.

After five minutes, he sees a guy in a black suit standing next to Cuues Marketplace, casually looking for something. It seems suspicious to Zadarion. He thinks about yesterday and what happened at his grandfather's place—about how strange Grandpa Jones was acting. He ignores the man and decides to visit his grandfather. Zadarion shows respect and knocks on the door. This time, Grandpa Jones answers right away. Zadarion walks inside.

ZADARION. *Looking dusty because of his fall.* Do you have some disinfectant or alcohol wipes for this bruise, Grandpa? I scraped my knee. If Mom sees this, she will go nuts.

GRANDPA JEDEDIAH JONES. There should be some in the comfort room.

ZADARION. *Turning his body around and facing his grandfather.* You mean the bathroom?

GRANDPA JEDEDIAH JONES. Yes.

Zadarion turns around, shaking his head a little. He walks down the hall and enters the bathroom. He decides to shut the door and apply the disinfectant on his cut.

ZADARION. *Dabbing alcohol on his bruise and thinking out loud.* First he drops his cane in the middle of the floor and ends up in the kitchen. Now he's calling the potty the comfort room. What happened to his version called the loo? *Finishes cleaning up his wound.* Mom and Dad said a while ago that he doesn't have Alzheimer's or dementia. What is going on? *Exits the bathroom and goes into the kitchen.* So, Grandpa, what's up?

GRANDPA JEDEDIAH JONES. This leg is killing me. Why not donate yours to me?

ZADARION. *Leaning on the countertop and starting to smile.* Yeah right, old man. *Laughs.* You better ask your son. *Laughing at his own joke.*

GRANDPA JEDEDIAH JONES. *Laughing.* Are you thirsty?

ZADARION. That depends. You have anything but carrot or prune juice?

GRANDPA JEDEDIAH JONES. I have Rémy Martin.

ZADARION. What's that?

GRANDPA JEDEDIAH JONES. Never mind. *Takes out a bottle of water.* Just have some fresh water. *Tosses the bottle to Zadarion.*

ZADARION. *Surprised by the unexpected toss, and the bottled water lands on the floor. He picks it up.* Some throw.

The telephone rings, and Grandpa Jones answers it. Zadarion glances once and, later, diverts his attention to the television, before noticing the time.

ZADARION. Oh! I gotta go. I will ... *Something is off. He looks at how his grandfather is talking on the phone.* I will see you later.

Zadarion leaves his grandfather's home, once again feeling something isn't quite right. At home at the dinner table, Zadarion, Mrs. Jones, and baby Kiley are having dinner. Zadarion plays with his food, his mind clearly occupied elsewhere.

MRS. HAILIE JONES. Something wrong, sweetie?

ZADARION. *He is quiet.*

MRS. HAILIE JONES. *Clearing her throat.* Ahem. *Looks quite serious.*

ZADARION. *Jumping in his seat.* I'm good!

MRS. HAILIE JONES. You sure? Because it look like something's bothering you. Talk to me, Zadarion.

ZADARION. Well ... *Puts his fork down.* Grandpa seems different.

MRS. HAILIE JONES, *spooning pieces of broccoli into her mouth.* Different how?

ZADARION. Yesterday night when I left Grandpa's house, I forgot to say good night. So I went back into his house. I found his cane on the floor, and he was in the kitchen leaning on a chair. Plus today, he called the potty room the comfort room. Who says that?

MRS. HAILIE JONES, *chewing her food slowly, takes a minute to reply.* That is strange. *Wipes her mouth with a cloth.* Maybe he's having an off day.

ZADARION. Yeah maybe. *Hesitates before adding more.* Hey, Mom, what if I told you I think Grandpa was abducted by three black-suited men I saw in town?

MRS. HAILIE JONES, *looking somewhat serious.* I would say, what would the government want with our Grandpa Jones?

ZADARION. Yeah.

MRS. HAILIE JONES. You look like you're through eating. Why don't you go and get some rest. You have a karate tournament this week, and I don't want you to be too tired doing those crazy moves your dad calls a sport.

ZADARION, *laughs as he gets out of his chair and takes his plate to the sink.* Okay, Mom.

Zadarion walks up to his room, changes out of his dirty clothes, and puts on clean pajamas to go to bed in. Zadarion notices a silver, metallic band on the upper part of his right arm. He did not notice before when he came home, took a shower, and went down to eat. The silver, metallic band had been invisible before.

ZADARION, *his eyes going wide.* What in the world? *Tries pulling the band off.* Stuck huh? How did this get—? *He remembers tripping over an object when he was walking home. He says out loud to himself.* How did this get on my arm?

Because he is beyond tired, Zadarion ignores the band for the moment. He goes into the bathroom, take a five minute shower then goes to bed.

Wednesday, April 12, 2107

The next morning the silver, metallic band is still on Zadarion's arm. Zadarion thinks about telling his mother, but he decides it's best not to tell anyone. Zadarion thinks that, if the government finds out … he'll be a lab rat. He also assumes that maybe he's mutating, thanks to his overactive imagination. Zadarion changes into his school clothes and walks downstairs.

MRS. HAILIE JONES. Hey, my little champion fighter! You all ready for tomorrow? *Placing baby Kiley in her highchair.*

ZADARION. Oh yeah. Just wish I didn't have school today. I have Mr. Colusson today. He sucks. *He lies. Mr. Colussen is one of his favorite teachers. He sticks up for him.*

MRS. HAILIE JONES, *smirking.* You sound just like your father. He used to say the same things back when we were in school. You have a great day today. Oh, Dad promises he'll be at your match tomorrow.

ZADARION. Yeah, well we'll see. Later, Mom. *Grabs his book bag and walks out the door.*

It's another long day that seems to be getting much slower as it goes. Zadarion finally leaves Mr. Colusson's class and walks to his locker. Dave Mikaelson intentionally bumps into him, and he falls on the floor next to his locker. Dave, Rich, and Mitch all walk away laughing. A boy with spiky red and black hair walks into a chemistry lab after witnessing what happened to Zadarion, and a girl who always stays to herself walks out of the school heading home. Zadarion stands up, and Sam hands him his book bag.

SAM KERRY. You all right, brother?

ZADARION. Why were they even born? *Opens his locker and exchanges a physics book with a quantum theories book.*

SAM KERRY. To be butt holes.

ZADARION. Yeah, you're probably right. *Closes his locker.* Your mom giving you a ride again?

SAM KERRY. Yeah, but later because I have chess club. Hey, you have that karate tournament tomorrow, right?

ZADARION. Yup!

SAM KERRY. If I hadn't injured my leg, I would be facing you this year.

ZADARION. There's always next year. You're joining again, right?

SAM KERRY. Mhm. *Smiles.* Hey, don't forget …this Saturday.

ZADARION. Nahhhh, I won't forget, brother.

The two friends shake hands and go their separate ways. Zadarion is walking through the city. On his way home, he gets knocked backward on his rear by a powerful but invisible wind. However, the people in the area around him felt no wind, and they are looking at him lying on the ground, confusion on their faces. Zadarion hears a voice whisper in his right ear, "Zada."

ZADARION. Grandpa!? *Looks around while pulling himself into a sitting position. In the distance, he sees a guy wearing a black suit entering an alley nearby.* Oh hell no. *Gets off the ground and runs toward the alley.* Hey, you!

The guy in black turns around. He's standing beside two others. Zadarion stands, facing the man, his fists tightened.

ZADARION. Okay, tell me why every time I see one of you guys, my grandfather says something to me that doesn't sound like the real him?

The guys in black suits exchange looks and then look back at Zadarion.

GRUNT 1. Turn around and leave son.

ZADARION. Why don't you tell me where you took my real grandfather?

Just before they turned around to depart, a wind lifts up Zadarion's right sleeve, revealing an object the men in black suits were sent to retrieve.

GRUNT 2. Where'd you get that?

ZADARION. How about from your mom's house.

GRUNT 3. Teach him some manners and take it from him. Brat won't remember us anyway.

GRUNT 1. Let's just get what we came for. *Charges at Zadarion.*

ZADARION. Oh, you guys wanna play. *Dives to the ground.*

GRUNT 1, *misses and smashes into a trashcan.*

GRUNT 3, *swings his fists at Zadarion.*

ZADARION, *swiftly dodging each punch, his mind on his karate tournament coming up.* That's all you got.

Grunt 2 comes up behind Zadarion, Grunt 1 close on his tail, and Zadarion instinctively falls to the ground. Zadarion rolls on the ground and picks up a trash can lid. He blocks a kick delivered by Grunt 2 and a punch from Grunt 3. Zadarion jumps back, and Grunt 1 grabs him from behind. As Grunt 2 approaches, Zadarion kicks forward. Grunt 2 successfully dodges the kick but slips on a puddle and falls. Zadarion head butts Grunt 1 in the face. When Grunt 1 drops him, he picks up the trash can lid once again and throws it at an approaching Grunt 3. Grunt 2 gets on his feet and sneaks up behind Zadarion, but Zadarion unintentionally throws his fist backward, knocking Grunt 2 unconscious. Grunt 3 stands in front of Zadarion, and Grunt 1 is behind him. They charge at him. Zadarion gets ready. Zadarion is blasted into a pile of trash; Grunts 3 and 1 are, at the same time, knocked quickly to the ground by an unseen newcomer. Grunts 1 and 3 pick themselves off the ground and go over to an unconscious Grunt 2, and the three teleport away. Zadarion crawls out of the trash and tries to look up at the approaching figure before losing consciousness.

Zadarion wakes up in an all-white room, feeling like he's been lying around for days. He gets off the bed and exits the room. He wanders around the strange facility, looking for an exit. Surprisingly to Zadarion, who thinks he was abducted, he sees no guards. He realizes he made this assessment too soon, as he hears voices coming his way. Zadarion hides in a nearby operating room, where he bumps into someone. He doesn't realize that he's looking at an important figure. But he will soon learn that this is, Thomas Jeffery Addams, commander of a secret agency called VLORs.

Commander Addams is in his early thirties, he could easily pass for a young man in his early twenties. Addams is all about VLORs. He has short hair, colored black and brown. He likes to look his best and to look different. There is nothing unusual about his persona.

Commander Addams. Well, hello there.

Zadarion. Uh-uh … Where am I? How'd I get here?

Commander Addams. You're at a highly advanced secret organization called VLORs. I had you brought here after your run-in with VICE grunts. *Walks toward the main computer and quietly speaks to a service operator so Zadarion cannot hear what he is saying.*

Zadarion, *looking around at all the equipment.* I'm where? Why did you bring me here?

Commander Addams. Oh I didn't. One of my special task force agents brought you. In all honesty, I had the agent watching you after ... *Walks past Zadarion, lifting up Zada's right sleeve with his index finger just as the room doors open, and he leaves the room.*

ZADARION. Wait! *Follows Addams.* Where's my grandfather? And who are you people? And what are you here to do?

COMMANDER ADDAMS, *stopping and turning to face Zadarion.* The reason you're here will be explained to you in due time. *Taps a button on his headset.* Commander Addams to Agent Caj. Meet me in Hall A near Room 2122. *Taps the headset off.* One of my agents will be assigned to get you properly adjusted to VLORs.

ZADARION. Wait! You're recruiting me? Why? Who are you people?

AGENT CAJ, *approaching Commander Addams.* Yes, sir.

COMMANDER ADDAMS. Yes, take the new recruit to the Center. You know what to do from there. *Departs down the hall.*

AGENT CAJ. Yes, sir. *Walks up to Zadarion.*

ZADARION, *backing away.* Waaaait, hold on. Who are you and what are you doing?

AGENT CAJ, *calmly placing his right hand on Zadarion's shoulder before grabbing him and shocking him with a jolt of electricity coming from the device on his right arm.* Relax. This is only to calm you down. Now rest. *Sighs. While Zadarion is sleeping, he says out loud to himself.* He was worse than that girl who I brought on board a few days ago.

Agent Caj has VLORs faculty take Zadarion, who is sleeping at the moment, to the Center. The Center is where all new recruits are sent. There, they will give their consent and start their training. The Center instructs them on everything they need to know. Zadarion wakes up within twenty minutes.

AGENT CAJ, *leaning on the wall next to the door.* Well look who's finally awake. You gon' freak out again?

ZADARION, *getting off the bed and rubbing his head.* You gonna shock me again?

AGENT CAJ, *laughs.* Sorry about that, little man.

ZADARION. What is this place? You realize it is illegal to hold someone against their will, right?

AGENT CAJ. You're not being held against your will. You're here because you've been selected to become a part of something great. You witnessed VICE grunts trespassing within your sector looking for who knows what. They might or might not have your grandfather. Who knows? Commander Addams instructed me to keep an eye on you because he noticed you twice having a run-in with VICE grunts. *Laughs.* I gotta hand it to you though, kid. You served up some sweet justice on their butts. Those moves were very nice. You got potential.

ZADARION. Thanks. *Wonders how Caj knew about his grandfather but does not mention to Caj that he thought he saw his grandfather's head vanish down an alley. Walks closer to Caj.* You said I'm not being held against my will. So I can leave?

AGENT CAJ. Sure, you can leave. *Steps aside.* But since those three grunts saw your face, they will be coming after you. *Walks in front of Zadarion and stops, facing him.* If I were you, I would at least give this place a chance and learn how you can get your grandfather back. *Walks out of the room and waits in the hallway.*

ZADARION, *thinking for a moment and then speaking to himself.* I know he was taken in that alley. *Quickly makes up his mind. Walks out of the room and sees Agent Caj standing on his left.*

AGENT CAJ, *smiling.* I knew you would make the right choice. *Extends his hand.* My friends on the outside call me Jack, but do not get into the habit of calling me by my first name.

ZADARION, *shaking Jack's hand.* Zadarion.

AGENT CAJ. Unique name. Follow me.

Agent Caj takes Zadarion to a room down the hall from the Center.

ZADARION. Where are we now?

AGENT CAJ. Before we start your training, there's this little thing called paperwork. It involves your consent.

ZADARION. I have to say yes, and that's it?

AGENT CAJ. That and sign the necessary form. Yes, that's it. *Walks into the office.* Hey, Angela, what's up?

ANGELA RUNN, *smiling.* Hey, Cajgie, is this our newest recruit?

AGENT CAJ, *leaning on the table that's right beside the entrance desk.* Uh huh. *Nods to Zadarion.* Zadarion, go stand over there and get ready to recite the oath.

The automatic door to the office shuts, and a monitor drops down in front of Zadarion. The monitor turns itself on, and none other than Head Commander Addams's face is being shown on screen.

VOICE. Please position yourself behind the line on the floor.

AGENT CAJ, *whispering to Zadarion.* Over on your left.

ZADARION, *looks down and makes his way behind the line.*

VOICE. Thank you. Please state your name.

ZADARION, *gulping.* My name is Ry–. *He pauses for a second.* Zadarion Jones.

VOICE. Thank You. Please repeat all that you see on the screen. Begin!

ZADARION, *taking a deep breath.* I, Zadarion Jones, do solemnly swear to support and defend the VLORs agency against all enemies that are foreign, domestic, or alien; that I will bear true faith and allegiance; and that I will obey the orders of the head commander of this here agency, VLORs, and the orders of the higher agents appointed over me. So help me, I will remain faithful to this cause until the bitter end or have my full memory erased permanently. *Tilts his head back.* Wait what?

AGENT CAJ. Aaaaand here comes the finisher.

ZADARION, *his right hand goes flying to his left arm, after he noticed a machine lowering down and had stuck a needle in his arm to collect a blood sample. Then the machine wraps a bandage around it.* Ow!

AGENT CAJ, *shaking his head.* I didn't like that either. *Makes a disgusted face.* Just necessary.

ZADARION, *rubbing his now bandaged arm.* Am I done?

ANGELA RUNN. Just about. *Walks to his side holding a paper and a pen.* This document states your immediate release from VLORs in case of a serious threat or a serious injury. This means that, in case you are hurt in any way, you forfeit your chances to continue being an agent of VLORs. You will thus have your memory erased, and no further knowledge of this world (of what we do) will you remember. Please sign.

ZADARION, *grabbing the pen and staring at Agent Caj.* Uh?

AGENT CAJ. Just simple information, and vitally important.

ZADARION, *signs the form.*

ANGELA RUNN. Thank you. Welcome to VLORs, Agent Z. *Smiles and walks back to her desk. She puts away the form, which will soon get logged into the computer system. The computer screen floats up and disappears in the opening in the ceiling.*

AGENT CAJ, *walking Zadarion out of the office and into the first training room.* All right, the first and second requirements of this training session test your physical skills and your mental capacities. The third is weapons training. You will not have time to do that today. These tests are pretty simple in the beginning. *He looks straight at Zadarion, holding his gaze for a moment.* Now, these tests never end. Once you officially become an agent of VLORs, you will continually have tests to help maintain your physical fitness and other skills. We want you intact and prepared for an imminent threat. (*Points to the door and then walks off but turns around.*) Oh and try to speed through this because you only got two hours before you have to be back home. Later, Z man. (*Departs.*)

Zadarion walks into the room and meets a droid, who immediately begins giving him training instructions.

PHYSICAL READINESS DROID. Hello and welcome to the physical training regimen. Today's training will be a simulation of an actual mission. You will be given the tools to deliver an outstanding performance. However, how you choose to use the tools depends on you. Each person has a unique style. If you step to your right, we will begin by setting you up with the training arsenal.

ZADARION, *walking over to the spot.* Okay, now what?

A transparent, circular tube comes out of nowhere and encloses itself around Zadarion. Zadarion's clothing is replaced by a white, fitted T-shirt and baggy, white cargo pants. His tennis shoes have been replaced with all-black combat boots. A metallic silver belt, which includes a black, boxed-shaped belt buckle, wraps around Zadarion's waist. Zadarion's curly hair becomes straight and extends upward, giving him a new look. Finally, as white gloves cover both of his hands, a device wraps around Zadarion's arm. The transparent tube opens up, and Zadarion walks out, admiring the awesome gear.

AGENT Z. Oh yeeeaaahhh. This is awesome!

PHYSICAL READINESS DROID, *gliding across the room in front of Z.* Whenever you feel ready, please stand completely motionless and repeat these words: "Simulation begin." *Glides to a corner.*

AGENT Z, *watching the droid position itself in a corner and then taking a deep breath.* Simulation begin.

The surroundings change shape, and Z is now standing on the side of gas station. Z peeks out and sees two drug dealers transacting a sale. As Z is carefully watching, his headset beeps.

AGENT Z. Whoa? *Feels the left side of his ear.* I didn't know I had this. *Clicks the button on the side of his headset.*

The headset gives information about the drug lords and suggestions on how to go about arresting them.

AGENT Z. Soooooooo. I'm supposed to ...? *Is completely lost about how to begin.*

The drug lords are both hard-looking criminals. Drug Lord 1 is wearing a leather jacket with a snake symbol on the back, and Drug Lord 2 has on a jeans jacket with rips on each side. Z decides to approach the two guys and talk with them.

AGENT Z, *massaging both wrists while smiling at them both.* Well, well, well. What do we have here?

DRUG LORD 1. What the hell you doing here, kid? Scram, will ya.

AGENT Z. I'll scram when your mother buys you some new clothes.

DRUG LORD 2, *pulling out his gun.* You don't want this … Just go away.

AGENT Z. You would shoot a kid! What a punk!

DRUG LORD 2. That's *it*! *Shoots five rounds at Z.*

Z instinctively cowers behind the broken-down car on his left. Drug Lord 1 pulls out his gun and starts shooting at the car.

AGENT Z. Crap! Okay, that's too much gunfire. *Considers how to engage.*

The two Drug Lords stop firing and reload their guns. Z jumps out from behind the damaged car and runs straight at them. He punches the Drug Lords out quickly, and the simulation ends. The droid glides closer to Z.

PHYSICAL READINESS DROID. Score of 55 out of 100. Displays of sarcasm, less effective. Little to no analysis occurred. Subject would have possibly been injured if enemy had endless amounts of ammo. A second simulation is needed in order to pass level. When ready, repeat the words, "Simulation begin." *Glides back to the corner.*

AGENT Z. Ah, come on. Give me a break. *Sighs.* Simulation begin.

AGENT CAJ, *loudly.* Simulation *over*! Override. Agent Caj! *Walks toward Z.* Man, what are you doing?

Agent Z. Training?

Agent Caj. I made this mistake before but worse during my first try. Listen, when the droid says, "When ready," do not begin the simulation unless you're sure that you are ready. You have time to prepare. Look through the files on your headset. Prep first and then begin the simulation so you can get the gist of it. You never want to jump headfirst into a fight. Trust me. *Taps Zadarion's shoulder before exiting the room.*

Agent Z. Prep first, huh? *Taps the headset on and learns how to summon weapons. He skims through some readings about proper ways to apprehend enemy targets.*

Agent Caj, *watching from outside the room.* Come on, little man. You got this.

Agent Z. All right. Let's try this again. Simulation begin.

Once again, the room changes shape. Z is hiding out in what appears to be a concrete tube. As he peeks out, he sees a scientist standing by a computer. He notices armed guards standing by all the exits. He sees a test subject that looks like it's being experimented on. Z takes a deep breath and figures out a plan. He calls out his blaster and gets ready.

Agent Z, *peeks once more over the guards' heads and sees an electrical line. Shoots the electrical lines over each door, and they fall on the guards, electrocuting the guards. Even though the guards were just electrocuted, he runs up to each one and punches every last one of them until he is sure they are unconscious. He targets the scientist's computer, intending to shoot the control box but mistakenly confuses the wrong machine for the control box.* Crap!

The scientist shoots at Z. Z cowers. The scientist then dives toward the control box and activates his test subject. The robot breaks its bindings and makes its way toward Z. Z fires the blaster at the robot's legs, but it barely scratches them up. The robot kicks at Z. Z dives under the robot and fires multiple shots from underneath. The robot cries out and falls backward. Z stands up and tackles the robot. When he stands on top of it the simulation ends.

PHYSICAL READINESS DROID, *gliding toward Z.* Score of 85 of 100. No displays of sarcasm or unnecessary commentary this time; a lot more effective. Average analysis occurred. Subject targeted the electrical wires without taking into consideration the possibility of the entire laboratory catching fire. Use of physical agility is well above average. Work is needed on firing skills and gun handling. Second simulation accessed and passed. Until next time. *Glides back to the corner of the room.*

AGENT Z, *speaking in a disgusted tone.* An 85? Ah, come onnnn?

AGENT CAJ, *applauding while entering the room.* Good job, Z. Don't mind that score. It's exceptional. Believe me; you do not want a perfect score. You need something that can be improved upon down the road. *Walks Z out of the room.* They prepared you a station. Walk with me. I'll take you there.

Caj takes Z to the main floor. They pass the recreational facilities and stop in front of the cafeteria.

AGENT Z. So, where are we?

AGENT CAJ. What do you mean?

AGENT Z. Are we inside a building or some big underground secret base?

AGENT CAJ. Not quite. *Sighs.* VLORs is sort of like a "ship." The ship is unknown, never seen before, and is believed to be mobile. There are two floors (passageways) on board VLORs. *Points down the hallway.* We're on the first floor. It's exactly the same above our heads, on the second floor.

Agent Z, *staring down both hallways.* Oh!

Agent Caj. Well ... *Lowers his arm.* You see, VLORs has two floors, Hall A and Hall B. I know I am repeating myself. Just follow along. Hall A is the first floor. The rooms are numbered from 2118 through 2122. This floor serves all personnel of VLORs. The Center, where you signed the form, is a training room for all new and current agents. Angela Runn is in charge of this space. The Geared'NReady room is a place where all personnel teleport in or out when coming to or leaving VLORs. The Main Control room is the place where service operatives find disturbances in the world. This is a place where meetings are held. Now, Hall B is above our heads, located on the second floor. The rooms are numbered 3118 through 3122. That hall also serves all personnel of VLORs. The Infirmary Ward is a hospital room to heal any wounds VLORs agents may have received in battle. There are a few top secret VLORs scientists, The VLORs medical team, who utilize new medical practices and new healing medicines. The Infirmary Ward has two rooms, 3118 and 3119. The other rooms, 3120 through 3122, are for the scientists of VLORs. These three WorkHouse rooms are experimentation laboratories. *Grows quiet for a while.*

Agent Z, *reading Caj's expression.* What's wrong?

Agent Caj. I didn't wish to mention what I'm about to say next. You see, I was not around when it happened.

Agent Z. When what happened?

Agent Caj. VLORs went by another name a few years before I came on board.

Agent Z. What was this place called then?

Agent Caj. VLORICE.

AGENT Z, *doesn't respond, but his left brow raises up.*

AGENT CAJ. Yeah. Commander Addams told me VICE split from VLORs. They were separate departments, but VLORICE was still one. VICE detached itself from the side bulkhead. The space has been repaired. You cannot even tell the difference anymore. The section VICE was in had two floors too. Hall A, located on the first floor, had five rooms, 2114 through 2118. One of those rooms was the Access'NGo room—a place where all personnel teleported in and out when coming to or leaving VLORICE. The other was a transport room. The Main Control was a miniature operations room, similar to but smaller than ours. This was the place where the commanders would congregate, a place where meetings were held. Hall B, located on the second floor, had five rooms, 3114 through 3118. These rooms served only the scientists. Now earlier, I mention "WorkHouse rooms", well there were more. These other WorkHouse rooms were also experimentation laboratories. There were five rooms in the hallway from what I was told. This hallway served all personnel of VLORICE. The Infirmary Ward was a second hospital room to heal any wounds important personnel—meaning the scientists and the commanders—may have received in battle. Commander Addams told me about a hidden space on this floor, but no one could not open it. (*Laughs.*) If I had been present then, I would've gotten it open!

The two walk to another room and enter the room where agents prep for their missions.

AGENT CAJ. This here you can call the Geared'NReady. You won't necessarily need to use these facilities much. I just thought I would show you where everything is located. So, what you think?

AGENT Z, *recalling his score from the training.* An 85?

AGENT CAJ, *laughing.* Seriously, Poindexter, don't get mad at that score. But for real, how you like it so far?

AGENT Z. It's wicked cool! When is my first mission?

AGENT CAJ. Once Commander Addams has one for you. Oh …you got the V-Link right?"

AGENT Z. You mean this? *Points to the headset.*

AGENT CAJ. Well, yeah, but that activates with this. *Points to a silver, metallic band with a touchpad screen located on his wrist.* This is what gets you in and out of this place. It's your V-Link—a device capable of transforming you into your agent gear. Each one is unique to each agent here at VLORs. You remember the blood sample taken from you?

AGENT Z. Yeah.

AGENT CAJ. This has that uniqueness that is encoded within your DNA structure. The device teleports your body, meaning it disintegrates your body into tiny particles and moves those particles from any location and finally to the VLORs base. That being said, no one knows where VLORs is located. I heard it's constantly moving. That may be a lie. I, to this day, have never seen the outside of the building.

AGENT Z. Wow. A V-Link huh. Anything else it does?

AGENT CAJ. Just transporting, activating your suit, and communication with VLORs. That's it. Oh it also has a cloaking mechanism, meaning it will go invisible when it needs to. Don't worry, Z. You will figure out how to summon your unique weapons in due time—of course after you pass weapons training.

AGENT Z. Can I finish it up now?

AGENT CAJ. I believe you have to be getting home soon.

AGENT Z. Right. Well, tomorrow after school and before my karate tournament, I will come back and finish all my training. The sooner, the better. I have to find those guys who took my grandfather.

Agent Caj. Right. Get the training done as soon as possible.

Agent Z. So, how do I get home?

Agent Caj. Just think it. With the V-Link strapped to your wrist, it is connected to your nervous system. Focus and think about your home or VLORs, and *presto*, you're there. Try not to tell anyone about today too.

Agent Z. Well, today was fun. I'll be seeing you. Later. *Concentrates on his house and teleports there.*

Agent Caj makes his way to the commander's office and knocks on his door. He is instructed to go inside.

Commander Addams. How was training day?

Agent Caj. Perfecto. There was no reaction from the device on his right arm either. I didn't pick up any kind of frequency with my V-Link; nor did I see it. You say it is on him, right?

Commander Addams. Correct, Caj. VLORs has been following that frequency for a long time now. A few days ago…*His eyes dart around the room, as if he's trying to be sure no one is listening.* …the mysterious device's frequency disappeared. At the last area where we picked up the frequency, VLORs surveillance cameras found Zadarion sitting on the ground after he'd tripped and scraped his knee. I figured it attached itself onto Zadarion's body somehow.

Agent Caj. I'll continue to monitor him. *Lowers his head.* Seriously, Commander. I just don't get it. What's so fascinating about it?

Commander Addams. I'm not quite sure. I've been given specific information about that mysterious device. After so many years on this planet, it finally found a host. *Glances up at nothing and then back down at Caj.* Just report anything unusual.

AGENT CAJ. Will do, sir.

The two exit the commander's office, and each goes down a different hallway.

Meanwhile, Zadarion successfully arrives home, having been transported into his bedroom.

ZADARION, *looks at the spot where the V-Link is supposedly attached to his arm. Right now, the mysterious device has cloaked itself. Zadarion decides to forget about it and focus on what's important. He has a karate tournament coming up soon, and now he can finally deal with his bullies. But first, he'll deal with the three guys in black suits.* This is so cool. If those guys in black suits make a comeback, I will be there to stop them. *Laughs and then stops and thinks about his grandfather.* Something tells me they took my grandfather, and I am definitely going to find out for sure that imposter is not him.

Season 1, Episode 2

Thursday, April 13, 2107

The next morning was pretty much a normal day for Zadarion. His classes went by quickly. After school, Zadarion and other young teens are preparing for their upcoming matches in the gym at the recreational hall, located in Kale County, IL. They prepare for thirty minutes individually. After the time has passed, the coaches summon their students as the host begins to announce the upcoming matches. The matches are divided into two categories. Over sixty students are registered, and they are split into two matches. Zadarion, along with others around his age group, are placed in the second match.

After an hour has passed, the first match ends and the winner is an older kid, two years older than Zadarion. The champion is put into the second round. As the second group is called down to the ring, everyone in the audience quiets down. The match begins. Zadarion glances up into the audience and sees only his mother cheering for him. Zadarion is disappointed that, even though his father promised to show up, he isn't here. Zadarion becomes distracted, and someone is gunning for him. Zadarion hears a silent footstep coming from behind him, and he raises his left arm upward and avoids the high kick with a blocking move. Zadarion turns his body and punches the young kid in the abdomen and then throws another punch to the boy's upper torso. The kid falls to the floor and taps out. Zadarion prepares for the others. The match is in its final twenty minutes.

At some point during the first ten minutes of the match, Zadarion's father walks in and sits beside his wife.

Many of the skilled children, who possess great techniques, eventually tap out. It is down to Zadarion and three others, including the champion from the first round. The audience watches as the remaining four target the older kid first, but two of them are

33

outmatched and soon tap out. Zadarion gets knocked on his back a few times, along with another kid. When the older kid finally makes the other kid tap out, Zadarion gets up and outsmarts him. He is quick. The older kid swings this way and that, and Zadarion ducks low and dodges each swing. Zadarion jumps high and kicks the older kid in the chest. Surprisingly, Zadarion is the one to fall, not the other kid. Zadarion falls on his back but manages to get back to his feet. Even though the older kid did not fall, he is weakening. Zadarion has his fists up, ready to end this. He glances up and sees his dad rooting for him. This hypes him up. The older kid notices that Zadarion is distracted and swings, but Zadarion raises his right arm and blocks. Then he counters with a left jab to the kid's jaw. The older kid became dizzy. Zadarion yells and jumps high, kicking him down using both feet. The older kid falls, and Zadarion pounces up and stands over him, extending his fist into the air. The referee calls the match and holds up Zadarion's left arm. Zadarion has won the state championships.

After the commencement ceremony, all the participants are handed awards for their hard work in making it to the state finals. Zadarion is beyond proud and is surprised that he has won. Little does Zadarion know, he is gaining confidence that he will need in the very near future.

DAVE JONES, *running toward his son and raising him high in the air.* That's my boy! Yeeeeeeeaaaaaaaahhhhh!

MRS. HAILIE JONES, *smiles happily.*

DAVE JONES, *placing Zadarion back down on the ground.* Look at you. State champion. How's it feel, son?

ZADARION. Darn good! *Smiles big.*

After the event, Dave takes his family out to eat at an Italian restaurant in Gradelia City, IL, driving first to the babysitter's mom's house to pick up Kiley. The house is a block away from Dave's home. Gradelia

City was built in 2020, with a goal of combining many cultures all in one. Instead, the city ended up becoming a major tourist attraction, gaining more restaurants after 2030. Today, the city boasts many different restaurants from every culture in the world.

The babysitter, Stacy, is a sixteen-year-old scholar student. Stacy is trying to raise money for college. It's her dream to get a college education and become a bioengineer. She also dreams of becoming an actress while in college. Stacy helps out other families, along with the Jones family, who need assistance in babysitting and home care.

After eating with his family at May's Italia Restaurant, Dave receives an important telephone call from a potential client about an out-of-town conference. He drives his family home and leaves for the airport.

The next school day, Mitch, Dave, and Rich met Zadarion at his locker at the end of the day, being jerks as usual.

MITCH CONALD. Little boy Zaddy won his little match. Shocking, it is.

RICH DAVIS BLOOME, *laughing.* Isn't it?

DAVE MIKAELSON, *trying to provoke Zadarion.* Hit me! Come on. Do it! *Slaps Zadarion's books out of his hands.*

All the students who are in the vicinity stop and stare at the trio messing with Zadarion, and they do absolutely nothing but watch. There is no sign of the spiky-haired boy and the quiet girl in the crowd of students. Zadarion's friend, Sam Kerry, walks up.

Sam Kerry, *picking up Zadarion's books from the floor.* Why don't you guys get a life?

Dave Mikaelson. Hold up. *Pushes Sam against Zadarion's locker.* Excuse me?

Dave Mikaelson is slowly approaching Sam Kerry, who remains pressed against the locker. Dave Mikaelson grabs Sam's shirt.

Zadarion, *getting in between Sam and Dave.* Leave him alone!

Before he even realizes what's happening, Zadarion has shoved Dave Mikaelson. Rich and Mitch look at Dave to see what he will do next. Dave charges at Zadarion and throws a punch. The principal shouts and grabs Dave's arm before Dave makes contact.

PRINCIPAL HARVIEL. That's it, Mr. David. Last strike. *Walks Dave toward the principal's office. Turns back to the other students and calls to them loudly.* I want all of you students to disperse now! *Looks at Dave.* No talking your way out of this, young man.

JANITOR MARVELLO. Where do you two think you're going? *Grabs Mitch and Rich by their shirt collars.* You still instigating, aren't you Rich? A ringleader, eh? *Groans.* Let's go.

ZADARION. You okay, Sam?

SAM KERRY. I'm good, but are you?

ZADARION. He didn't hurt me much. *Gathers his belongings.* Let's get out of here.

The two walk out of the school building and go to the kindergarten play area, where they sit and wait for Sam's mom to pick him up. After thirty minutes, Sam leaves with his mom, and Zadarion walks home. Making his way down the street, he passes many stores on the way home. Suddenly, he is snatched into a seemingly dark alleyway. A tall African American male slams Zadarion hard against a brick wall.

ZADARION, *groans.*

GRUNT 3 (NICK). Remember me, punk? *Grips Zadarion's shirt collar tightly, holding him up against the wall.*

GRUNT 1 (TED). Let him go, Nick! Calm yourself.

GRUNT 3 (NICK). Made me look like a weakling the other day. *Growls in Zadarion's face.*

ZADARION, *trying to avoid the awful smell coming from Nick's mouth.* Duuude.

GRUNT 2 (PEDRO), *placing his hand on Nick's right arm.* Put him down, Nick.

NICK, *turning his head to the left.* Make me, Pedro.

GRUNT 1 (TED). Come on, Nick. Our orders aren't to kill him yet.

GRUNT 3 (NICK), *turning his head away from Pedro and to his other side and then groaning.* You're a coward, Ted. *Turns back to face Zadarion, and his grip on Zadarion's shirt collar tightens. His fists feel like they are pressing against Zadarion's neck.*

GRUNT 1 (TED). I didn't want to have to do this, Nick. *He does a roundhouse kick, striking Nick in his back.*

NICK, *drops Zadarion immediately and falls to one knee.* Argh, I'll kill you, Ted!

ZADARION, *having flipped away from them when he fell, stands up, massaging his neck.* Big gorilla.

GRUNT 2 (PEDRO). Focus, Nick. *Points at Zadarion.* We came for that device on the kid's arm.

GRUNT 3 (NICK), *standing up.* Argh. Then after... *looks at Zadarion with murderous eyes* ... he's mine!

GRUNT 1 (TED). Sure. Whatever. Let's just get that device for Commander Talgitx first.

ZADARION, *stops rubbing his neck.* So you guys wanna play some more. Lucky for you, I got some new tricks. *Thinks about his agent form, and his V-Link activates. The agent clothing appears on him, and this time he's wearing a jacket. The headset speaks to him, instructing him to initiate the Invisi-Dome.* Invisi-what? Oh, all right.

GRUNT 1(TED), *looking closely, intrigued.* Oh shit!

All three grunts charge toward Z at once. Z runs straight at them and flips over them. He tosses up his right hand, and a beam of light shoots out of his hand and surrounds the area in an invisible dome-like barrier.

The Invisi-Dome is a technical strategy used by agents, mostly agents of VLORs, to secure the area so no pedestrians get hurt. It's also undetectable by any outsiders. The Invisi-Dome has properties to restore a damaged city.

GRUNT 3 (NICK). You brat. *Charges at Z again and swings his fists.* I'm going to squash you, you bug!

AGENT Z, *dodging each swing delivered by Nick and then starts jumping backward.* Heheh.

GRUNT 2 (PEDRO), *pulling out his small blaster.* Smile at this. *Shoots lasers at Z.*

AGENT Z, *jumping once more and, this time, landing on top of a fire escape ladder.* You guys can do better than that.

GRUNT 1(TED), *throws a trash can at Z.*

AGENT Z. Uh-oh. *Jumps down.*

Nick runs and tries to catch Z, but Z twists his body and swings his foot at Nick, kicking him across his face. Nick gets knocked into a trash can. Pedro charges at Z, still firing his small blaster. Z dodges by running from side to side, and he tries to uppercut Pedro. Pedro blocks the attempt and unintentionally drops his weapon in the process. Z and Pedro go back and forth, each throwing a lot of punches in his opponent's direction, but both are blocking the other's punches. Ted runs up behind Z, but Z ducks low. Ted swings and accidentally punches Pedro. Z raises his leg up and kicks Ted in the gut. Z grabs Pedro's small blaster, jumps up high, and shoots Pedro. Pedro hits the brick wall and falls into a pile of trash. Nick appears behind Z with both arms raised up high, but Z rolls sideways and shoots the fire escape ladder. The ladder lands on Nick's head. Nick is seeing stars. Z takes aim and slings Pedro's small blaster at him. Just as Pedro is getting back to his feet, the blaster clocks him in the head, and he falls back on the ground. Ted comes out of nowhere, kicking randomly at Z. Z dodges each kick and leans backward. Z kicks Ted's other foot, and Ted trips. With the force of power in the agent suit, Z grabs Ted's leg and throws him into a brick wall. Nick returns, and Z quickly punches him in his face. Z's headset beeps. He receives a call from VLORs. The trio tries to get away.

AGENT Z, *noticing that the trio is trying to escape.* No! Hold it right there! *The headset instructs him about V-Cuffs, and V-Cuffs appear in his right hand.*

V-Cuffs are small, round, and a slick piece of metal that opens into a spiral and binds around an enemy to immobilize the person.

GRUNT 1 (TED), *attempts to run out of the Invisi-Dome.*

AGENT Z, *speaking quietly.* Why doesn't he teleport like last time? *Throws one pair of V-Cuffs at Ted and then another at Nick. He loses sight of Pedro.* Now where did the other one go?

Pedro is nowhere to be seen. He is hiding somewhere close, waiting for Z to leave the area. Once Z leaves the area, the Invisi-Dome will lift and he'll be able to leave. Ted and Nick are lying down on the ground, completely immobilized thanks to the V-Cuffs.

AGENT Z, *looking down at Ted and Nick.* Wow. Cool. (*Laughs.*) That was really fun! (*Tunes in when his headset beeps again.*)

The headset alerts him to return to VLORs at once. Z clicks his headset off. He focuses on the VLORs headquarters and teleports, taking Ted and Nick along with him. Z gets to VLORs within 0.05 seconds, arriving in the Geared'NReady room. He walks out into the hall and makes his way to the main control room. The double doors open, and Z sees Commander Addams speaking with a service operator, who's sitting at one of the control operations desks.

COMMANDER ADDAMS, *turning to face Z.* Ah. Good evening, Agent Z. *Signals the service operator to continue working and then directs his attention to Z.*

AGENT Z, *standing straight, his arms at his side.* Sir.

COMMANDER ADDAMS. At ease, son.

AGENT Z, *relaxing his body.* Yes, sir. *Breathes out.* What's up?

COMMANDER ADDAMS. I apologize about you being attacked, but hey, congrats on your capture of the two VICE grunts. *Gives Z a thumbs-up.* Good job. Oh and please raise your score in weapons training.

AGENT Z. Yes. Well about that, sir. I was in a hurry because I thought I would miss this important event that I already had plans to attend.

COMMANDER ADDAMS. I see. Well, like I said, get that score up. (*Lightly smiles.*) I'll be watching you. *Walks past Z and out of the room.*

Agent Z. Yes, sir.

Z leaves the room too and walks in the opposite direction the commander went, heading toward the recreational room. Along the way, he is filled with the excitement of his first successful enemy capture. Even though it was not a mission given to him, it felt sort of like retaliation. Plus, he is still confused about this thing called VICE. Z is walking down a hallway on the second floor, his head literally held high. He lowers his head looking ahead and sees a girl about his age walking toward him. This is the most beautiful girl he has ever seen. Her arms are crossed. He can almost hear angelic bells. In his mind, white lights are emanating from this girl, who is wearing the typical all-white pre-agent gear. He is at a loss for words. He is mesmerized. The two young agents pass one another, each taking a quick glance at the other. After passing the attractive girl, Z continues walking forward but turns around and is now walking backward. He watches the girl, who is now walking away from him, as she turns the corner to the next hall. Z bumps into someone and quickly turns around.

Agent Caj. Well, if it isn't the Zerminatorrrr! (*Laughs.*) Nice capture. So whatcha lookin' at, man?

Agent Z, *stuttering.* Uh. (*Quickly turns around for a second and then faces Caj again.*) No one.

Agent Caj, *knowingly.* I see you met Agent Rahz.

Agent Z, *Whispering to himself.* Agent Rahz. (*He looks at Caj.*) How long she been here?

Agent Caj. Since about a few days before you came. Let me tell you, Z. Her training scores are … (*Whistles.*) I was shocked how she handled those scientists in her simulation. You might have a rival there.

Agent Z, *getting cocky.* Pfft … (*Lets out a cocky, if slightly nervous laugh.*)

AGENT CAJ. Where you headed?

AGENT Z. I was going to go to the recreational room, but now I want to go to weapons training to raise my score. Then I'm going to go home for today, I mean unless they assign me a mission or whatever.

AGENT CAJ. Cool. Well, I'll be seeing you. Later, Z man. (*Departs down the hallway.*)

AGENT Z. *Looks thoughtful as he watches Caj leave and then turns toward the simulation training, and mutters aloud.* She is pretty.

Pedro teleports to the VICE headquarters, located somewhere in Kale County, IL. He makes his way to the commander's office. The secretary invites him inside the main office and informs the general he has a visitor. An older man in his early fifties welcomes Pedro into his office.

GENERAL TALGITX. Have a seat. (*Points to a chair.*)

PEDRO. Thank you, Commander, sir. (*Sits down.*)

GENERAL TALGITX. I personally prefer *General*. Thank you.

PEDRO, *nervously.* Sorry, General, sir.

GENERAL TALGITX, *standing and walking to a window.* No need to be nervous, son. So why have you come to my office?

PEDRO. Well you see, sir. Ted and Nick, my fellow VICE agents, have been captured by VLORs. VLORs has a new agent, sir. He is wearing that device ...you were ...looking for.

GENERAL TALGITX. *He stares out the window, keeping his back toward Pedro. He whips around, facing Pedro, his lips pursed, and then stand straight there, as if staring straight through him, an angry look on his face.*

PEDRO. Sir?

GENERAL TALGITX. I believe you would like another chance to redeem yourself?

PEDRO. That would be great, sir.

GENERAL TALGITX, *turning from the window and walking to his wine collection, he avoids eye contact with Agent Pedro and prepares himself a drink.* Would you care for a drink?

PEDRO, *standing up and facing General Talgitx.* Yes, si— I mean, no thank you.

GENERAL TALGITX, *taking a sip from his glass.* Go. New instructions will be given to you by the secretary outside my office. You may leave now.

PEDRO, *bowing.* Thank you, sir. I will not let you down again. (*Leaves General Talgitx's office.*)

GENERAL TALGITX, *waiting until Pedro has closed the door to his office.* No, you won't. (*Places his glass down but picks it up again.*) Human soldiers are worthless. *Breaks the glass in his hands.*

Pedro meets with the secretary, grabs his orders from her, and he walks out of the main office doors.

Saturday, April 15, 2107

The next morning, Zadarion wakes up in his bed feeling refreshed and thinks his muscles are tighter. He checks himself out in the mirror with his shirt off and flexes his arms. His mother opens his bedroom door, telling him to place his laundry in the laundry room for wash on Sunday. Today is Saturday. Zadarion forgot to place his laundry in the laundry room Friday night. Zadarion gathers all his dirty clothes and takes them down to the laundry room. He thinks about his grandfather and that promise he made to himself to find out the truth. Zadarion puts on a shirt, grabs a snack, and runs out the door. He is stopped by his mother's voice.

MRS. HAILIE JONES. And where are you going young man? (*Fastens the baby in her highchair.*)

ZADARION. To meet Sam. We're going to see that new movie, *Blaine Idol IV.*

MRS. HAILIE JONES. You're going now? This morning?

ZADARION. It's ten in the morning, Mom. But nah, first we're going to the arcade.

MRS. HAILIE JONES. All right, sweetie. Have fun. Be safe.

ZADARION. I will. Later, Mom. (*Walks out the door.*)

Zadarion has lied about going to the arcade and, instead, makes his way to his Grandpa Jones's house. Zadarion arrives at Grandpa Jones's house and knocks on the door. His grandfather opens the door for him to come inside. Zadarion steps inside, massaging his wrist.

ZADARION, *looks around, expecting to see something odd or out of place.*

GRANDPA JEDEDIAH JONES, *eyeing his grandson.* Looking for something, son?

ZADARION. Why don't you tell me?

GRANDPA JEDEDIAH JONES, *laughing and then turning around and heading into the kitchen.* You still hungry?

ZADARION, *following behind him.* Nah, I'm good. (*Sits on the stool by the counter.*)

GRANDPA JEDEDIAH JONES. What time are you meeting Sam at the movies? I can give you a ride.

ZADARION, *clearly shocked that his grandpa knew about his plans.* In a few hours. But me and Sam decided to stop by the arcade first.

GRANDPA JEDEDIAH JONES. I remember when I was your age. (*Sighs and then turns to face Zadarion and looks up at the ceiling.*) Me and old man Archibald were quite like you and Sam.

ZADARION, *looking at his grandfather and smiling wide because he caught him.* Ha! I knew it! (*Gets off the stool.*) Funny. I thought you told me before how you met Archibald in college?

GRANDPA JEDEDIAH JONES, *looking worried.* Uh?

ZADARION. Uh. (*Laughs.*) I know you're a phony. Who are you? (*Walks to the window.*)

GRANDPA JEDEDIAH JONES, *laughing a little.* What are you talking about, Zadarion?

ZADARION, *turning around.* Don't play dumb, you doppelganger. Where's my real grandfather?

GRANDPA JEDEDIAH JONES. Are you sick, son? You feeling all right?

ZADARION, *picks up an object quickly and throws it at his grandfather's cane, causing the cane to fall to the floor.*

GRANDPA JEDEDIAH JONES. What's the matter with you? (*Bends down, without any trouble, to pick up the cane.*)

ZADARION. Need help? (*Smiles.*)

GRANDPA JEDEDIAH JONES. Nah I'm go— (*Stops short, realizing his mistake and is quiet.*)

ZADARION. Nice posture, Grandpa. (*Maintains his smile.*)

IMPOSTER GRANDPA JEDEDIAH JONES, *standing up straight.* All right. What I do wrong?

ZADARION, *speaking in a disgruntled tone.* Everything. (*Activates his V-Link and transforms.*) You're about to tell me where my real grandpa is.

IMPOSTER GRANDPA JEDEDIAH JONES, *looks confused.*

AGENT Z, *takes a step forward, the spectral light glowing in his hand.*

IMPOSTER GRANDPA JEDEDIAH JONES. No! (*His form cracks, and the crack heals itself.*)

The imposter posing as Zadarion's grandfather launches at Z, attempting to smack the device emitting spectral light out of Z's hand so Z cannot summon the Invisi-Dome, as that would prevent him from escaping. Z pulls his hand back, and the imposter knees Z in his stomach. The spectral light fades away, and the device falls to the floor and vanishes. The imposter raises both his hands and slams them down. Z rolls on the floor to avoid the blow. He sweep kicks the imposter's legs, and the imposter falls on his back. Z slams his right fist at the imposter's face, but the imposter grabs Z's hand. Z punches the imposter with his other hand and hurts his hand.

AGENT Z. Ow! (*Rolls on the ground away from the imposter.*) What are you made of?

The imposter gets off the ground, Zadarion see that his face is chipped, and light seems to be coming from inside it. It is not healing this time. Zadarion's mouth drops.

ZADARION. I repeat. What are you?

IMPOSTER GRANDPA JEDEDIAH JONES. I am your grandfather.

ZADARION, *shakes his left wrist, and his gun appears. Points it at the imposter.* Who are you?

Feeling threatened, the imposter acts violently and charges at Zadarion, moving at extreme speed. He throws Zadarion at the kitchen counter. Zadarion drops his weapon. The imposter speeds out of the house quickly. Zadarion gets up but is struggling.

ZADARION. No, no, no, no, no! Dammit. (*His headset beeps, and he clicks the button.*) Zadarion here.

AGENT CAJ, *having teleported, appears beside Z and taps his headset off.* What the hell happened here?

AGENT Z. Something kidnapped my grandfather and was pretending to be him. I found out and… *Shaking his head in disbelief and a little confused.* … this.

AGENT CAJ, *looking around the room and seeing a light sparkle on the floor, walks over and picks up the tiny fragment.* A repliara cystatite.

AGENT Z. What's that?

AGENT CAJ. A piece of— (*Stops short*) I'll explain it at VLORs. Meet me there. (*Teleports away.*)

AGENT Z, *changes back into his normal attire and walks over to the front door. Checks outside and sees that all appears normal.* Grandpa, I swear I will find you. (*Closes the door, changes back into his agent attire, and teleports to VLORs.*

Z arrives at VLORs within 0.05 seconds in the Geared'NReady room. He walks to the main control room. Z, who is facing an unhappy Commander Addams, stands up straight.

AGENT Z. Sir, I— (*Stops upon hearing a tiny noise from Caj and looks at the agent.*)

AGENT CAJ, *shaking his head at Z.* Shhhh.

COMMANDER ADDAMS. No, please, let him talk. I would like to know *why* he would target someone without being given a direct order. (*Lowers his tone.*) Well, Z?

AGENT Z, *looking at the floor and then at Commander Addams.* Well you see … (*Places his hands in his pockets.*) Something was pretending to be my grandfather, and I wanted to expose that fake! *He takes his hands out of his pockets, quickly.* You made me an agent to stop bad people, right?

COMMANDER ADDAMS. The point is you do not act on your own. If he hadn't escaped, what do you think would've happened to you?

AGENT Z, *looking frightened and then looking down at the floor.* I don't know, sir.

COMMANDER ADDAMS. Precisely. *Breathes out. He speaks out loud to everyone in the room, including the service operators who are sitting at their work stations.* How on earth did a VICE grunt acquire a repliara cystatite?

AGENT CAJ. Sir, I don't know. But the real question is… *Takes a glance at Agent Z.* …what was it doing posing as the kid's grandfather?

COMMANDER ADDAMS. You're right, Caj. (*Looks at Z.*) Make sure that, next time, you contact a member of VLORs before you go on a dangerous mission, no make that any mission.

AGENT Z. Yes, sir. (*Looks displeased at having just been yelled at.*)

Commander Addams instructed Caj to have Z meet with Alexander Torres, and he leaves the room. Caj walks over to Z, who feels beaten down.

AGENT CAJ. Hey, Z man. Don't feel that way. He didn't mean it. But that was dangerous. You could've died. Next time, call an operator and let them know you found something suspicious. And ask whether you should proceed in an attack.

AGENT Z. Sorry. (*Breathes in and out deeply.*) So, who's this Alexander Torres?

AGENT CAJ. A martial arts specialist. He's trained in a lot of fighting styles and knows a lot of techniques. Addams wants his new recruits trained fully before engaging with any members of VICE.

Caj takes Z down to the Center. As they arrive at the double doors, Z turns to Agent Caj.

AGENT Z. When will you guys tell me about this VICE and what they want with my grandfather?

AGENT CAJ, *letting out a small chuckle.* You see, the thing is, we don't even know. What I can tell you is that VICE was inactive for almost a year. The moment we discovered VICEs reappearance was when we found you. You were the first one to see members of VICE in a long time. This means that they're making a comeback. They're planning something.

AGENT Z. Oh. (*Thinks about the grandpa clone.*) What about the VICE grunt who was pretending to be my grandfather. Was he a robot?

AGENT CAJ. I wish I could show you that piece of repliara crystatite. Upon my arrival, I gave it to scientists down in the laboratory to be examined. They destroyed it. The repliara crystatite is a scientists' invention. The creator is unknown. But it can encode any physical qualities of a person, turning them into a clone of the person of the user's choice. I have never fought anyone using this technology before. But I read about it in our database.

AGENT Z. I guess it has superstrength capabilities, right?

AGENT CAJ. That's right. How'd you know?

AGENT Z, *rubbing his shoulder.* The thing threw me.

AGENT CAJ. Least you're okay. That's what matters. Next time, you'll be ready for it!

The doors open, and Alexander Torres steps out to greet them.

ALEXANDER TORRES. Is this my new punching bag, Cajgie?

AGENT CAJ. This is the new *recruit*, yes!

ALEXANDER TORRES. Sorry to hear about your reckless behavior, Z. If I hadn't been out of town, I could've trained you sooner so that you would've been better prepared. (*Nods at Caj.*) Oh and, Caj, who was that girl you sent me this morning? (*Smiles.*) She was ...*mannn!* After she told me she had no karate experience, I wasn't expecting her to be that good. (*Looks down at Z.*) Maybe I should stop training teens.

AGENT CAJ, *laughing.* Yeah— (*Stops when his headset beeps.*) Looks like Commander Addams wants me. Z man, kick his butt, all right? (*Departs down the hall, answering the call as he goes.*)

AGENT Z. Heh heh.

ALEXANDER TORRES. Well ...don't be shy. Come in.

AGENT Z. I'm never shy. After you. (*Follows Alexander into the training room.*)

While Alexander starts Z's advanced training, Caj is sent to check out a distress call. He teleports to an empty field, where a laboratory has burned down.

AGENT CAJ. It looks like I'm too late. (*Walks over rubble and broken pieces of concrete.*) No signs of life or any active technology. It's all been destroyed. *He sees a body lying twenty feet from him and runs over to check on the person. He runs his V-Link over the body and looks at the readout. He mutters to himself, looking perplexed.* Diagnostics check out. *He helps the guy up.* Come on, buddy. Hey wait. I know you?

PEDRO. Please. Let me die here. (*Pushes Caj back.*)

AGENT CAJ, *confused.* Now why would VICE leave one of their own? (*Grabs Pedro.*) Sorry bro, I can't leave you.

PEDRO, *yelling in a tone that is both angry and frightened.* No! You don't understand! (*Struggles.*) Let me *go!* If they find me ...they'll, they'll ...

Caj hears footsteps approaching. Before he has a chance to act, he is blasted fifty feet away from Pedro. By the time Caj makes it back to the spot where he found Pedro trying to commit suicide, both Pedro and whoever fired the blast are gone. A cleanup team of VLORs arrives to clean the area.

AGENT CAJ. Dammit. *Looks around and, after carefully searching, taps his headset.* Agent Caj to VLORs to Commander Addams. *Makes contact.* There's nothing here. Whatever they found, they got it. But there's something more. I will tell you upon my arrival. Agent Caj out. *He teleports away from the stark scene.*

Caj returns to VLORs, and after he talks with Commander Addams, the two discover that Pedro went rogue. He had no affiliation with the destroyed laboratory. He hid there to commit suicide. They also discover that an electronic emitter (something that creates endless amounts of electricity) was being created there. The scientists that worked on it had all been taken by VICE. The burned corpses were dummies, all fake. What could VICE be doing? What would they construct with the electronic emitter?

Tuesday, May 2, 2107

Agent Z has spent two weeks training with one of the world's best fighters, and he's worked hard to master Alexander's suggested techniques. Agent Z's training got off to a rough start. Z, remembering his plans with Sam, rushed out after the first hour of training. He had to go. Besides seeing the awesome trilogy, Blaine Idol IV, the friends had another important motive – going to the movie would give them a chance to talk to Sam's crush.

Despite Z's success in the rigorous training by Alexander Torres, Z still has trouble in weapons training. He handles sharp objects in his own personal style, which is why he hasn't passed weapons training. Z holds his sword in a way that is different than he's been trained. He wins his share of battles, yes …but sooner or later he will not be so lucky.

After the training with Alexander Torres, Z is placed on his first assignment. Z is placed on an assignment to apprehend two thugs for attempted robbery of an oil refinery. The thugs have managed to get away with a few tanks of oil. The stolen oil is a special blend that has been experimented on by a scientist believed to be working for VICE. The thugs placed the special oil in a truck and fled the scene after seeing Z sneaking around. Using his new flight board, Z caught them as they headed out of Dower's City, IL, making their way toward Kale County. As they near an abandoned lot, Agent Z put up an Invisi-Dome, in which he is now fighting the thugs. He already has one thug wrapped inside a spiral V-Cuff, and he is rapidly dodging gunfire from the other thug.

Z swoops down on his flight board (which is raised to avoid the gunfire) and aims right at the thug. The thug is knocked on the ground as Z flies past. Z hops off his board (it folds away and dematerializes). The thug reaches for his gun, but Z kicks the gun far away from him. Angry, the thug jumps to his feet, punching wildly at Z. Z dodges, ducking low and moving side to side. He uppercuts the thug and extends his leg, kicking the thug to the ground.

AGENT Z. End of the road for you, buddy.

SNAKE. *He quickly pulls out a small object, aiming it at Z, and sending a blindingly bright light in Z's direction.* That's what you think. *Runs away to hide and calling over his shoulder as he disappears.* No one catches Snake.

AGENT Z, *blinking and rubbing his eyes as his sight returns, looks around and concludes that the thug has escaped.* Least I got yo boy. *Turns and faces the immobilized thug.* Looks like Snake abandoned you. Aw, so sowwy. *Taps his headset and calls VLORs.* Agent Z to Co. Addams. Are you there?

COMMANDER ADDAMS, *on his headset at VLORs.* I'm here. What do you have to report?

AGENT Z. A thug calling himself Snake blinded me for a second and escaped. I have his partner and the special blend of experimented oil that was stolen from the refinery. They're being transported now.

COMMANDER ADDAMS. Good job, Agent. Keep it up. (*Ends the call.*)

AGENT Z, *tapping his headset off and watching as the oil and the captured thug are transported to VLORs.* I gotta find a place to change back. (*Finds a convenient place to transform back into his normal clothes.*)

Meanwhile, Snake (who apparently did not go far) walks out from behind a building.

SNAKE. I gotta get that oil back somehow. (*Kicks the air.*) Damn!

A figure approaches Snake, revealing himself to be a scientist. The two discuss a plan that will ensure Snake isn't punished for his failure. If he were to return to VICE without the special blend of oil, he would regret it. The scientist suggests that Snake follow him. They get inside a car and head for the scientist's home. Snake and the scientist (who is none other than Scientist Kelo Ritz) arrive at a local residence on Gravers Street (in Dowers City). They get out of the car and go inside the house.

Kelo Ritz is a mysterious scientist and a creepy individual. Though he is elderly, one should never drop his or her guard with the man. He has his way around things, and somehow he knows everything about a person.

SNAKE, *looking around.* This is your lab?

SCIENTIST KELO RITZ, *chuckles and then does something Snake can't see to make the lab entrance appear.* Let's move.

Scientist Ritz immediately activates a big, bulky, and unknown machine, as Snake watches in the distance. Ritz goes to a cabinet and he grabs a jar that contains snake DNA (an indication that he has been planning to experiment on Ray "Snake" Gardner at some point). Kelo has an unusual smile on his face. He looks happy and almost like there's an ulterior motive.

SNAKE. What's that?

SCIENTIST RITZ. Your future. (*Looks excited and thrilled.*) Please position yourself on that table. *He points at the table.*

SNAKE. Uh. Hold up. I never said anything about being a lab rat. *He steps backward, shaking his head adamantly.*

SCIENTIST RITZ. Fine. Leave. Let VICE find you. We'll see what they do to you after failing to sec—

SNAKE. All *Right*! (*Looks at the examination table.*) Will it hurt?

SCIENTIST RITZ. You'll be fine.

SNAKE, *pointing his finger in Ritz's face.* I better become stronger than that agent. If you turn me into a freak, I swear … (*Growls angrily.*)

SCIENTIST RITZ, *looking rather calm.* Are you done?

SNAKE. Yeah. Whatever. (*Lays on the table.*)

Hooks bind Snake onto the table to prevent him from moving. Ritz adds the snake DNA in the machine. Ritz grabs a needle and injects Snake with a stabilizing compound he created. The machine activates and lowers over Snake's body and charges power. Snake's body is fidgeting. He is responding positively to the snake's DNA. Ritz has an evil grin on his face. Snake's skin bubbles and pulses. Scales begin to form over his skin, overlapping one over the other. Soon, Snake has undergone a successful experiment. The binds release Snake from the exam table. He rises from the table and stands up, admiring his new scaly form. He is wearing no clothes. The skin resembles a skin tight suit but it's realistic. The scales and snake skin are almost real. Ritz uses a controller to activate a silent machine, which is behind Snake and straps a band around his arm. Snake growls at Ritz.

SCIENTIST RITZ. Uh, uh, uh. Tsk. Tsk. You work for me now. Attempt to disobey me, and I will obliterate you with this controller. If you attempt to take my controller, it will negatively affect you and will destroy itself. No more controller and you're permanently stuck that way. (*Grins.*)

SNAKE. You tricked me.

SCIENTIST RITZ. No. I helped you. (*Laughs and then flips a switch to light up the room, revealing large photos of other experiments on the walls.*)

Snake turns around and sees other mutants like himself. Most of them are mutilated. Scientist Ritz looks at Snake, his first successful creation of a specimen that has survived the process without mutilations.

Scientist Ritz. Congratulations. You're now a cross-human. Now let's talk about how to deal with Agent Z. *Tightens his fists.* I shall *not* have my plans foiled again by a VLORs agent.

What could Kelo Ritz possibly mean by *again*? Who stopped him before? As the scientist plots to one day finally outsmart VLORs, Zadarion makes it home and heads straight to bed early.

Wednesday, May 3, 2107

The next day, Sam Kerry surprises Zadarion waiting outside of his home. Together, they walk to school. Today, Centransdale High School, the school Sam and Zadarion both attend, will be welcoming a new student—Kiyla Gerald, who moved from the Dominican Republic last week and transfers schools quite often. Her mother had promised to keep her enrolled at Centransdale High for the rest of her high school years. Kiyla has relatives in Asian countries and in Hispanic countries and comes from a wealthy family. Kiyla is stuck-up, tends to act like a prissy, and can be a spoiled brat. Kiyla arrives in front of the school in a nice-looking SUV. She steps out, carrying her designer bag, and walks toward the door.

Kiyla Gerald, *pushing the double doors to the school open.* Centransdale students, beware. Kiyla has made her debut! (*Strikes a sassy pose.*)

Several students turn to look at her. They whisper, "freshman," and turn to continue their conversations. Kiyla smiles, walks to her newly assigned locker, and opens it. She looks to her right and sees an

African American girl sporting cute pink bangs. Kiyla closes her locker and introduces herself.

KIYLA GERALD. Hi! I like your hair. It's cute and stylish! (*Smiles invitingly.*) My name's Kiyla. (*Poses while describing herself.*) The one. The finest. The truest. (*Stops posing and extends her hand.*)

JAYLA PRICE, *smiling and blushing a little.* Thank you. (*Keeps smiling.*) You're such a character. Ha ha. My name's Jayla Price. (*Shakes Kiyla's hand and then lets go.*) Welcome to Centransdale High. (*Smiles back invitingly.*)

KIYLA GERALD. Care to help me get adjusted to your school, Jayla? (*Gives off a cute pouty expression.*) Pleaseeee! (*Smiles.*)

JAYLA PRICE, *is surprised at how quickly she and this new girl have become friends.* Suuuuure. (*Telling a lie.*) I'm like the fashion guru princess around here.

KIYLA GERALD. I can see that, with your cute self. (*Looks Jayla up and down.*) Work it, sister girl.

JAYLA PRICE, *lets out a pleased laugh and spins a full 360 degrees.*

KIYLA GERALD. Jayla. (*Places her arm around Jayla's neck.*) We're going to own this school. Just you watch. The boys will flock to us, the girls will envy us, and the teachers will respect us. Trust me, Jayla. We are two fashion little miss missies. (*Takes her arm from around Jayla's neck and, grabbing her designer bag and wrapping it around her, looks around.*) So when does first period start?

JAYLA PRICE. In about thirty minutes. We're early. (*Wraps her arm around Kiyla's neck and smiles.*) Gives *me* time to show my new buddy where all her classes are. (*Holds her hand out for Kiyla's class schedule.*)

KIYLA GERALD, *hands Jayla the form.* Thanks, bestie!

The two girls walk down the hallway together. A while later, Zadarion and Sam enter the building and head to their lockers. They realize they only have six minutes to get to their lockers and quickly grab their things. Two minutes later, Zadarion and Sam head to first period. Along their way, they pass Jayla, who is showing Kiyla where her first period class is located. Sam turns around briefly and then turns back around, smiling at Zadarion. Sam and Zadarion doesn't see it, but Kiyla smiles at Zadarion when they pass.

KIYLA GERALD. Hmm, they are cute.

JAYLA PRICE, *smiles a little, aware of who Kiyla is talking about.* A bunch of losers, too.

KIYLA GERALD. Still. (*Looks at Jayla smiling.*) Unless he's already yours, or maybe you're jealous.

JAYLA PRICE. Pfft …pleeeease! (*Hides her tiny smile.*) Let's hurry and find your first period class.

ZADARION. Dude, what's so funny?

SAM KERRY. Nothing. (*Continues smiling.*)

ZADARION, *stops walking.* Dude. Seriously what?

SAM KERRY. Can't believe you passed the love of your life, man. (*Makes kissy faces at Zadarion.*)

ZADARION, *hiding his feelings.* Dude, it was a second grade crush. I'm over it. Besides, she's too popular now. (*Turns around, blushing a little.*) Let's hurry and get to first period before we're late.

Season 1, Episode 3

Wednesday, May 3, 2107, continued.

At an undisclosed location in Dowers City, IL, VICE has set up a warehouse, in which a select handful of scientists are collaborating on a project given to them by VICE commander General Talgitx. One of the scientists there is a young man who goes by the name Professor Dila. His real name is Lilori Daniels. Lilori is twenty-eight years old and a bit timid. His skills are in quantum mechanics and cosmology, and he specializes in space and time theories. For years, since his college days, Lilori has been secretly working on a side project—a unique teleporting device capable of jumping different dimensions that is not quite finished. At VICE, Lilori is underappreciated. His job with the organization is to build weaponry defenses. For many years, he has wondered whether there is life on other planets and whether there are other dimensions.

Lilori walks out of the break room. He's been having frequent headaches this past week and believes the cause is something that he experienced a month earlier. The exact date when the headaches started, subsiding shortly only to return three weeks later, was Monday, March 13, 2107. Lilori walks into his assigned lab and takes a seat at his desk. He looks out the window for a second and sees that it's nighttime. He looks at his blank computer screen and has a flashback:

> Lilori is traveling through space inside a tiny spaceship. He does not know where he is located, but he's in another galaxy—a galaxy that he never studied before in school. A flash of something is hurtling toward his ship. He cannot seem to make out the object. After the light passes his ship, a metal object of some kind emerges from the light. His ship starts to malfunction, and the passenger aboard is

freaking out. He notices another life form, but it's not him.

Lilori is now standing at a wreckage site. He sees something small crawling slowly away from the downed ship. When it has reached a safe distance, the creature turns its head, and the ship self-destructs. Lilori is now standing in his old laboratory, picking up files that have fallen to the floor. The date is Sunday, March 12, 2107. He hears a notification alert on his computer and goes to check it out. He is staring at his computer screen. An image suddenly appears, and Lilori sees a distorted alien life form. The creature materializes right in front of him. Its body is distorted.

Lilori wakes up and jerks his body back.

Lilori Daniels, *panting*. Was that a dream? (*Thinks back to that night.*) No. You're real. Aren't you?

A creature has been possessing Lilori, lying dormant in his mind since their meeting in Lilori's laboratory on Sunday, March 12, 2107. The distorted-looking alien, who fled planet Vegues for his crimes, managed to project itself inside Lilori's mind on March 12, 2107. Vegues is light-years away from Earth. A day after the incident, Lilori felt nothing unusual, except for the slight headaches that quickly subsided. But on Wednesday, May 3, 2107, while sitting at his desk in the warehouse, Lilori starts to feel different. His insides are getting hot. This pain subsides after thirty seconds. Then suddenly, a voice replies to the question he spoke out loud.

DıLuAH. What a peculiar human you are. You possess much intelligence up here. Your knowledge can be quite useful. Yes. But I wonder? Why did you not discover sooner that another life form has been slowly studying your mind from the inside? Hmm? A being of your stature would be highly expected to formulate a plan to eradicate another life form from its body. (*Grows quiet and remains so for a while.*) It is time for our merger to begin.

LILORI DANIELS, *falls to the floor.*

The truth is Lilori was fully aware of what fused with him a month ago. Since he had no side effects, other than the headaches, he figured it must've been an illusion, due to one of his inventions. DiLuAH apparently lost his physical form due to the crash and the close contact with that strange object in space. DiLuAH's body split apart, meaning half his body was lost in another dimension while the other half was in Earth's dimension. Also, DiLuAH's body can't survive long on any other planet. He needs a host body, especially in his current state. Lilori's body, especially his mind, was the perfect match. Lilori's body has been adjusting to DiLuAH's remaining cellular structure. After lying on the floor in pain, Lilori rises from the floor and clutches his desk. He feels new and stronger.

LILORI DANIELS, *standing up.* What's this? *He watches his skin changing a purple color.*

DiLuAH IN LILORI'S MIND. Our fusion is slowly becoming permanent. We are equal. Our minds are equal. Neither is superior. You and I will eventually know everything about the other. Do not be alarmed, Lilori. With our combined intelligence, we're invincible. *Sighs.* However, this process will take time to finish.

LILORI DANIELS. People will freak. I can't just walk around with purple skin. And what will we call—? (*Stops short, a smile crossing his face.*) I know. (*Looks up.*) The world shall soon know the two of us as, DiLusion.

DiLusion's new body is still undergoing changes. His skin is only a slight purple. But Lilori is already calling himself DiLusion. He wanders around the lab and then picks up the Dimension-Travel device that Lilori has been working on for years. Upon his touch, the device glows. It strangely adapts to DiLuAH's abilities—among which are his ability to create portals that lead into darkness and to teleport from one place to another. However, due to his body splitting in two, he lost this ability. Thanks to Lilori's invention, this will be remedied—the device will serve DiLusion as a means of transport. He, in this new combined form, will be able to teleport once again but in a slightly different way than before. DiLusion straps the device around his right wrist, and a portal opens up in front of him. He walks inside. The new place is dark and soundless. DiLusion sees the other half of DiLuAH's physical form, but strangely they are not combining together. DiLuAH's body is frozen, but not in ice. The other half of DiLuAH's physical form has been sent to this desolate dark dimension and is trapped with no way out. DiLusion decides to make this place his new home. DiLuAH swears to find a way to get his body back to normal.

Thursday, May 4, 2107

After spending a good amount of time in the desolate, dark dimension, DiLusion returns to the warehouse on Earth. It is now nine in the morning. General Talgitx is making a surprise visit to check on the progress of the latest invention—a "something" he personally ordered. DiLusion hears Talgitx's voice down the hall. He grins. Downstairs, Talgitx is admiring the developments that the other scientists have come up with. One of them—"teacher's pet"—approaches Talgitx.

SCIENTIST. Good morning, my fair general. How was your trip?

TALGITX. My travels were peaceful. Now, tell me ... Any news about the electronic emitter?

SCIENTIST. Yes, sir, wonderful news. The analysis was quite remarkable. This device was made with impenetrable carbonized steel—very tough. That and the endless supply of electricity it can create in vast quantities.

TALGITX. How is the duplication process? How many more have you copied?

SCIENTIST. Oh we have over 10,000,000 units so far, with more on the way.

TALGITX. That's exciting news.

DiLUSION. Isn't it though? (*Grins, eyeing them both and walking down the stairs.*)

The scientist and Talgitx both turn to see where the voice came from. Talgitx nods at the scientist to go back to his station and continue working. Talgitx approaches the staircase.

TALGITX. Ah, Lilori. Come to give me a report?

DiLUSION. Eh. Something like that. (*Walks around Talgitx and watches the other scientists hard at work. Turns to face the general.* I'm wondering. What are all these inventions for general? (*Grins.*)

TALGITX, *feeling that something is wrong with Lilori.* Conditions are causing great stress to affect your skin, I see.

DiLUSION. Just an experiment gone wrong. *(He smiles.)* So, what are we building?

TALGITX, *walking the few steps past Lilori and watching the other scientists.* A means to an end.

DiLUSION. Awww. How quaint. Quoting a philosophical work. Immanuel Kant's theory of morality?

TALGITX, *turning to face Lilori.* Precisely, my friend.

DiLUSION. Say someone were to expose this little facility. I suspect the end result would be disastrous, no?

TALGITX, *eyeing Lilori cautiously.* One would surely regret it to the highest authority. Are you feeling all right?

DiLUSION, *grinning.* I've never been more alive, General. (*Walks over to the scientist duplicating an electronic emitter.*) May I borrow this friend?

SCIENTIST, *looking slightly uneasy.* Sure. Go ahead.

DiLUSION, *watching the scientist with a smile and then examining the electronic emitter.* Ahh. Remarkable.

TALGITX, *walking up to the scientist and Lilori.* Professor Dila, don't you have work to get back to?

DiLUSION, *placing the electronic emitter on the table.* About that. You see, Talgitx. I have to say, I call it quits.

TALGITX. Come again?

DiLUSION. You heard right.

TALGITX, *raising his head up a little.* Ahh. Really?

Three VICE grunts approach the two, positioning themselves behind Lilori. DiLusion/Lilori faces Talgitx, grinning.

TALGITX. Now, care to repeat that last part, Mr. Dila?

DiLUSION, *looking serious.* It's DiLusion!

DiLusion fights off two VICE grunts and back kicks the third grunt in the abdomen. The third grunt smashes into a scientist's workstation and then rolls off the desk and onto the floor. Talgitx attempts to back away, but DiLusion grabs his shoulder. Talgitx grabs DiLusion's wrist and flips him over his shoulder onto the floor.

DiLusion. *He is getting off the floor and he's smiling.* Ah, commanding officer has secrets? Well, so do I.

DiLusion launches himself at Talgitx, who steps to the side and throws DiLusion into one of the scientist's work station. More VICE grunts arrive, and a couple of them barricade the exits, preventing DiLusion's escape.

DiLusion. You underestimate me, General.

VICE grunts charge at DiLusion to try and subdue him. DiLusion deals with them easily. He takes one of their blasters and shoots at the VICE grunts who are blocking the doors.

Meanwhile, General Talgitx is shouting to all other scientists to send all files worked on and currently being worked on to VICE corporate folder, HQ. DiLusion overhears this and shoots at each workstation.

Talgitx. Stop him! (*Picks up one injured VICE grunt by the arm and forces him to attack DiLusion.*)

DiLusion, *brutally knocks out each VICE grunt.* All ...too ...easy.

A VICE grunt gets in a sneak attack and punches Lilori in the back of the head. DiLusion turns around and shoots him across the room.

DiLusion. What a fool. (*Looks at Talgitx.*) Poor little general, losing his freshlings. (*Laughs.*)

Talgitx, *a questioning expression crossing his face.* Always knew you were a disturbed individual.

DiLusion. You don't know the half of it. (*Charges at Talgitx.*)

The two go blow for blow. Talgitx is really giving it his all, or at least he's making DiLusion believe he is. DiLusion and Talgitx punch each other, each blocking the other's punches. DiLusion strikes Talgitx in his upper right arm. Talgitx feels pain and quickly throws a punch toward DiLusion's right cheek. DiLusion smashes into a workstation. Talgitx holds his upper right arm and backs away to the exit doors. Three remaining uninjured VICE grunts get to their feet to protect Talgitx. Talgitx, annoyed at their many failures, pushes them away.

VICE GRUNT. Sir, you're hurt.

TALGITX. I don't need your pathetic help. (*Punches the grunt to the floor.*)

DiLusion, *laughing maniacally.* I *love* it! (*Gets off the ground and moves away from the damaged work station.*)

TALGITX, *still clutching his upper right arm.* You just made an enemy in VICE. Believe that, friend.

DiLusion. Oh, who gives a shit. (*Jumps on top of a workstation and crosses from station to station until he makes it to the high window.*) It looks like whatever experiment you've been concocting is hereby terminated. (*Laughs and then throws up the peace sign.*) Arrivederci! (*Shoots an exploding compound on the floor. Then, when a portal appears behind him, jumps backward and disappears into the portal. The portal closes.*)

TALGITX. That's what you think, freak. (*Angrily leaves the building, many scientists trailing behind him.*)

As the explosive compound explodes, destroying the warehouse, Talgitx and the scientists evacuate. They are teleported to VICE. A secretary standing outside Talgitx's office sees Talgitx holding his upper right arm.

MRS. JANET MULON. Oh my god, General. (*Stands up and walks out from behind her desk over to him.*) You need medical attention.

TALGITX. Call Mario Vega to my office, immediately.

MRS. JANET MULON. General, the mechanical brace on your arm has been damaged, hasn't it?

TALGITX. Just call him, Janet. (*Holds his upper right arm and walks into his office.*)

MRS. JANET MULON. Yes, General. (*Takes a seat at her desk again and calls Mario Vega on the intercom.*)

During the event at the VICE secret lab, Agent Z has been tracking down a fugitive who escaped from a bus that was headed to Primous Facility.

Primous Facility is located on Methphodollous Island, it's located somewhere close off the East Coast of the United States. Primous Facility is a facility that houses psychotic individuals (who have had mental breakdowns), hardened criminals, and the like; there is also talk of the facility being used to hold cross-humans.

His target, Max Gerald, is in his twenties and is a pyromaniac. Luckily, Z has found him and activated an Invisi-Dome before he was able to burn down Valousse City, IL.

MAX GERALD. Get back, kid! (*Brandishing the flamethrower unit he's holding.* And drop this freakin' barrier! (*Looks around, fidgety, and then at Z. Points the flamethrower at Z when Z makes a move.*) I mean it! Don't. Move!

AGENT Z. Relax. *Takes small steps toward Max, his hands up.* I just wanna help— (*Jumps up high and twirls in the air, thanks to the new gliding-rocket devices in his boots.*)

Max Gerald, *shooting flames where Z was standing and in the air.* Aaaahhhhhhhhhhhhhhhhhh!

Agent Z, *delivers a kick from out of the air, right into Max's chest.*

Max Gerald. Ah! (*Hits the ground and laughs.*)

Agent Z, *standing on the ground in front of Max.* You got buuuurned, dude.

When Max attempts to stand up, Z kicks Max back on the ground. Z flips his right wrist, and a V-Cuff materializes in his hand. Z throws the V-Cuff at Max, and the V-Cuff wraps around Max, immobilizing him. Z receives a call from VLORs.

Agent Z, *tapping his headset.* Yup! Z here.

Commander Addams. Great capture, Z. Oh. Make sure you deliver Anaheim's flamethrower unit safely back to him. Commander out.

Agent Z, *tapping his headset off.* Awww. I wanted to keep it. (*Picks up the flamethrower unit and examines it.*) This thing is awesome.

While Z is returning the stolen flamethrower unit to Curtis Anaheim at Anaheim Industries, Agent Caj is on Northern Beach in Oirailie Island, located on a Northern California peninsula. Northern Beach is clean and well kept. Caj proceeds to another spot. He discovers a hidden laboratory. According to files, the place exploded many years ago. There is nothing left but pieces of concrete and eroded metal slabs. It's a mystery. Caj explores the area, wondering why vegetation would grow everywhere else but right here. After walking around for several minutes and finding nothing unusual, Caj spots something sticking out of the dirt.

Agent Caj, *talking to himself.* I think I found something.

Caj jogs to the spot. He tosses an explosive device, a Q3 explosive— a sonic screech that clears away small particles like dirt, small rocks, and the like—and stands back. After the tiny explosion clears, he returns to the spot and discovers toys that have been buried. He scans the toys and discovers they're from old television cartoon shows. There is nothing else in the area. Caj communicates what he's found via headset to Commander Addams, hangs up, and teleports to VLORs. Walking down the hall, he passes Z.

AGENT CAJ. Eh. My main man Z. How are the missions you've been assigned going?

AGENT Z. They're good. I wish I could get missions like you're getting. I'm just arresting street thugs.

AGENT CAJ, *laughing—understands how Z is feeling.* Gotta start somewhere. You'll get them soon. But remember! Every mission is important. (*Changes the subject.*) Oh! How's your new robo-grandpa. Any suspicions from your folks?

AGENT Z. Nope. They think he's normal. (*Sighs.*)

AGENT CAJ. Remember. That's a good thing, Z. We don't want to draw suspicions.

AGENT Z, *not so excited.* Yeah, I guess.

AGENT CAJ. *He remembers he has to be somewhere.* Ah, man. I gotta go. (*Walks off.*) Later, Z man.

AGENT Z. All right. Later.

Friday, May 5, 2107

The next day after school, Zadarion meets Sam Kerry outside of the arcade, and the two walk inside. After two hours of playing

GrandSteel: Siege of Destruction, a character action fighting video game, Sam and Zada hop on the virtual motorcycles and race one another. Sam wins one round and taunts Zada. Zada wants a rematch. Sam looks over to the entrance and sees Jayla Price and Kiyla Gerald walking past the arcade. Sam nudges Zada.

SAM KERRY, *nudging Zada*. Looks like Jayla was about to come inside.

ZADARION, *jumping up and looking at the window*. What!?

SAM KERRY, *laughs and continues to play the game. His motorcycle passes Zada's*. Hahahaha!

ZADARION, *grinning*. Arrrgghh. You're dead! (*Gets back in the game*.)

Sam and Zadarion having been playing for about an hour when, just two blocks down the street from the arcade, a robot smashes up a building. A local pedestrian opens the doors to the arcade and shouts inside, "Hey everybody, *run*! Killer robot!" Sam hears people running and takes off the virtual reality helmet.

SAM KERRY, *pulling Zada's arm*. Zada, come on! We gotta go! *Now*!

ZADARION, *taking off the virtual helmet*. What? Why? (*Looks around*.) Where'd everybody go?

SAM KERRY, *yelling*. Let's get out of here!

Sam and Zadarion exit the arcade. Sam starts running away from the robot wreaking destruction while Zadarion stands staring at it, mesmerized. Sam runs to his friend.

SAM KERRY. Zada, let's go!

ZADARION. Yeah.

Zadarion starts running with Sam. When Sam turns a corner, Zadarion yells to Sam, "I'll catch up to you. Keep running. Don't stop, brother." Zada makes his way to an alley and transforms into his agent gear. Z throws up an Invisi-Dome and confronts the robot.

DOMETREAD. Get out of my path, puny human. (*Smashes a building to its left.*)

AGENT Z. Cut that *out!* (*Uses his V-Link to materialize his blaster.*) Drop your hammers, now! (*Points his blaster at the killer robot.*)

DOMETREAD. Never. (*Swings its massive hammer arms at Z.*)

AGENT Z, *flipping over the hammer arms.* I'm warning you. (*Shoots multiple shots at the robot.*)

DOMETREAD, *mad.* No one does that to DomeTread. (*Stomps its feet, creating seismic quakes.*)

AGENT Z. Oh heck no. (*Boots activate for gliding. Jumps and hangs from a flagpole and fires more shots at DomeTread.*)

DOMETREAD. Stop shooting me! (*Swings its hammer arms at Z.*)

Z swings off the flagpole, and DomeTread's attack misses its mark. Z launches at DomeTread, landing on the robot's head. DomeTread's head steams, and Z falls on the ground. While still lying on the ground, Z fires more shots from his blaster and then jumps to his feet. Before running away from the robot, Z kicks the robots left leg. Z runs and turns around. DomeTread becomes furious and goes on a rampage. The robot charges at Z. Z charges at DomeTread. DomeTread swings its hammer arms down toward the ground, hoping to smash them on Z's head, but Z rolls on the ground and runs under DomeTread. Z uses the gliding devices in his boots to jump high and delivers his best kick into

DomeTread's metallic back. DomeTread falls forward, and the ground shakes. Z lands on the ground, and a V-Cuff appears in his hand.

AGENT Z. Give up and stay down! (*Approaches cautiously.*)

DOMETREAD, *speaking like a prehistoric caveman.* DomeTread never gives up!

DomeTread gets to its knees and its left hammer arm ejects from its body and aims at Z. Z jumps high and dodges it, but the hammer arm ricochets back. Z is knocked on his face. The hammer arm reattaches onto DomeTread's body. DomeTread stands on its feet. Z stands up.

AGENT Z. Cheap shot. (*Spits on the ground.*)

DOMETREAD. Ha-Ha-Ha-Ha-Ha. Puny human fall down and get owie. Ha-Ha-Ha-Ha-Ha.

AGENT Z, *pulling out his sword.* Yeah, that's right. Keep laughing. (*Gets ready to attack.*)

Z charges at DomeTread, materializes his sword, and raises his sword high. He slams his sword at the robot's legs and dodges the hammer arm before it can strike him. Z swings his sword once more and strikes DomeTread's legs. DomeTread yells in pain and slams its hammer arms at the ground. Z jumps on and runs up DomeTread's arms. He smacks the sword across DomeTread's face and then glides off the robot and swings his right foot at its metallic cheek. Z lands on the ground and fires his blaster. The laser strikes DomeTread's torso and damages the shield plate covering its central core. DomeTread roars. The robot falls to its knees.

DOMETREAD. No, master. Not now. I must kill human kid. (*Is teleported away.*)

AGENT Z. No! Crap! (*Clicks his communicator on.*) Z coming aboard. (*Teleports to VLORs headquarters.*)

Z arrives at VLORs within 0.05 seconds and exits the Geared'NReady room, making his way to the control room. He approaches Agent Caj, who is just finished speaking with a VLORs operator.

AGENT CAJ. What is it, Z man?

AGENT Z, *looking around, admiring the equipment.* Oh yeah. I was just battling some robot called DomeTread. Hidendale Springs needs to be cleaned up, like *now*—before people start to discover that there are secret organizations out in the world.

AGENT CAJ, *smiling and nodding toward the main computer screen.* Check this out. Quickly, scan your V-Link there.

Z walks over to the main computer and scans his V-Link. The area where Z was fighting DomeTread, outside the arcade, is completely cleaned up. No debris remains.

AGENT Z, *looking at the screen and then at Caj.* But how?

AGENT CAJ, *pointing to the V-Link on Z's arm.* This has recording features and an Invisi-Dome is like a repairing system. Think of the Invisi-Domes as an alternate reality. No one can see you fighting inside of one. Pedestrians around the area no longer remember what occurred prior to you activating a dome. Yes, there was the little damage before you activated the dome, but after you activated it, no real damage was done to the area. VLORs also has the cleanup crew to clean up excess damages. Best be glad *you're* not on that duty.

AGENT Z, *admiring his V-Link even more.* Cool. (*Smiles.*)

AGENT CAJ. Why didn't you capture the robot?

AGENT Z, *jumping and looking at Caj.* Oh! Well some guy was communicating with it. The robot said, "No, master. Not now. I must kill human kid." It sounded like a caveman to be real. Then it was teleported away. Pretty weird.

AGENT CAJ. Appears there's a new scientist out and about. Be careful out there, Z.

AGENT Z. Oh fo' sho. (*Laughs.*) Next time I see DomeTread, that robot's coming back with me to VLORs.

Caj smiles. Then nodding to Z, he walks away. Z heads for home. Agent Rahz is walking around the corner, into the Geared'NReady room and stops at the door. Rahz watches Z teleport. She later does the same.

It's eight o'clock at night. Having taken a shower, eaten dinner, and brushed his teeth, Zada goes to his room and decides to call Sam to see if he's all right. The phone rings several times, and Sam finally answers.

SAM KERRY. Hey what's up, Zada?

ZADARION. Nothing. Just ate and lying in bed watching TV. Are you okay, though, after what happened today?

SAM KERRY. Uh, what are you talking about?

ZADARION. Come on, you know. At the arcade and what happened after.

SAM KERRY. Yeeeaahh ...you disappeared, and I went home. It's cool though. I'm not mad. I assumed your mom called you, and you had to get home fast. Don't sweat it.

ZADARION, *thinking about what actually happened.* Yeah. That's right. So, you finish your math homework?

SAM KERRY. Nope. Working on that now. Oh that reminds me. (*Laughs.*) If my mom hears me on the phone, that's my ass, man. I'll talk to you tomorrow. See you at school, brother.

ZADARION, *laughing.* Yeah, later brother.

Sam and Zadarion finish talking on the phone and hang up. Meanwhile, at a laboratory in VICE, a young shadow boy is secretly watching Dr. Machenist repairing DomeTread.

DR. MACHENIST, *fixing DomeTread's damages.* You have somewhere to be, Mr. Rodriguez?

JOEL RODRIGUEZ, *appearing to hang from the ceiling, his body a black shadow.* Nope. (*Drops to the floor.*) Another failed robot, I see. Tsk-tsk.

DR. MACHENIST. Just you wait, kid. You'll see soon enough. (*Changes the subject.*) If I were you, I would be more concerned about General Talgitx catching me snooping around VICE laboratories. (*Finishes the repairs and activates DomeTread, who walks to a corner of the laboratory and enters sleep mode.*)

JOEL RODRIGUEZ, *picking up a tool from a shelf to admire it and then placing it back on the shelf and facing Dr. Machenist.* You let me worry about General Talgitx, kay? (*Walks to the exit doors.*)

DR. MACHENIST. I know you heard about his distaste for cross-humans. Just looking out for you, Joel.

JOEL RODRIGUEZ. Thanks for the concern, but I'm okay. Talgitx doesn't scare me. Oh, and one last time, call me ShaVenger. (*Exits the laboratory.*)

DR. MACHENIST. Stay out of trouble, kid. (*Adds to himself.*) The first cross-human discovered. He better watch his back.

Dr. Machenist finishes up in his laboratory. He scans a new female robot model that is almost ready to go online and looks at an icy android beside the female model. Joel walks the halls of VICE and teleports to the rooftop of Hidendale Observatory. Joel lies on his back.

SHAVENGER, *gazing at the stars.* Tired of waiting. *Starts to daydream about the day of his accident.*

The year was 2103. Joel was eleven years old. He wandered into his stepfather's secret study room where his stepfather was doing an experiment. Both of them were caught in an explosion that cost Joel a temporary loss of his body and sent him to a desolate, dark dimension. Joel's body just faded away. Joel couldn't see anything. He prayed and wished he could see his mom again. Then one day he, without realizing how or even that he was doing it, teleported to his bedroom. Joel became a cross-human. After a month, Joel's body turned a dark black, and he discovered that he could teleport. Joel has often thought about taking revenge on his stepfather—not just for turning him into a monster but also for having replaced his deceased father. Joel, also known as ShaVenger, was taken to VICE. To this day, Joel sits patiently at VICE and waits. He sneaks out sometimes to watch the VLORs agents. Joel wakes up.

SHAVENGER, *still lying on the rooftop of Hidendale Observatory.* Just wait. I won't sit here for much longer.

Saturday, May 13, 2107

A whole week has past, and Zadarion has had one hell of a week. Today, it's almost noon, and Z is outside of Hidendale Observatory, fighting a lizard monster. Z whips out the new Vectra Boppers. The two of them have been fighting inside of an Invisi-Dome, and it's been thirty minutes. Neither Z nor the lizard monster knows that ShaVenger is sitting on top of the observatory watching the battle.

Z twirls his body, flying toward the lizard creature and kicks forward. The lizard creature smacks onto the pavement and then jumps back up.

SNAKE, *looking at Z.* You're gonna pay for last time. (*Points at Z.*)

AGENT Z, *looking confused.* What do you mean *last time*? I never fought you. You know, I'm starting to think *maybe* I bopped your ass a little too hard on the head.

SNAKE, *growling.* The oil.

AGENT Z, *his eyes go wide.* Oh, youuuuu! Wooowww. (*Looks the creature up and down and starts to laugh.*) You've gotten uglier. (*Laughing hysterically.*)

SNAKE, *growling.* You're gonna regret that statement. *Charges at Z.*

AGENT Z. Yeah right, lizard breath.

Z stands with both feet planted on the ground and both fists at his sides, waiting. Snake dashes at Z, throwing his fist straight at his target. Z blocks, using both his fists. Z pushes Snake back. Z launches forward, ducks low, and lands an uppercut. He jumps up high and knees Snake in the face. Snake falls on his back but quickly wraps his tail around Z's arm, flinging him up in the air. Snake claws at Z, ripping his pants.

AGENT Z. Hey! (*Gets mad and head butts Snake.*)

Snake has his eyes closed long enough for Z to use a lot of force and punch Snake's lights out. Snake squirms on the ground. Z approaches Snake, looking down at him.

SNAKE. You're gonna pay.

AGENT Z. Yeah right. (*Raises his Vactra boppers up high, but Snake throws dust in his eyes.*) Aaahh!

Vactra boppers are like boxing gloves but they pack a devastating, dynamic punch. They're made of soft but firm alloy.

SNAKE, *wrapping his tail around Z and squeezing tightly.* I told you that you would pay.

AGENT Z, *gasping for air.* Oh …this is …fair.

SNAKE, *punching Z in the face multiple times.* What…did…I…tell…you?

It looks as though Z is finally beaten. But Z starts laughing. Snake's punching stops.

SNAKE. What's so funny?

AGENT Z. You know, next time. (*Spits to his side.*) Don't just wrap *your stinkin' tail around my arms, idiot!* (*Quickly kicks Snake in the forbidden zone.*)

SNAKE, *an unpleasant look on his face.* That's …dirty …fighting. (*Falls to the ground.*)

AGENT Z, *freed from Snake's tail.* Pfft. Dirty, my ass. (*The Vactra boppers disappear, and a V-Cuff appears in his hand.* Have fun in— (*Hears a familiar noise close by and turns around.*)

The Invisi-Dome has been broken into. DomeTread, who's drilling from underneath surface, burst through the ground, returning for another round.

AGENT Z. Oh, this just isn't my day. (*Dodges DomeTread's swinging hammer arms.*)

DOMETREAD. Stop running, meat sack.

DomeTread slams its hammer-arms one at a time into the ground as Z dodges. Z summons the Vactra boppers again and punches DomeTread in the head. DomeTread throws the hammer arms up, and Z is flung into the air. DomeTread jumps off the ground, following Z. From in the air, Z dives down at DomeTread, his fists pointed down. The two clash. Z swings his right leg at DomeTread's face before falling to the ground. The Vactra boppers disappear, and Z materializes his blaster. Z points the blaster at DomeTread. DomeTread hits the ground and stands back up. Z shoots while running toward DomeTread. DomeTread holds up its hammer-arms. Z gets in close range and continues shooting. DomeTread is taking the hits, all the while swinging its hammer-arms at Z, trying to knock Z out. Z dodges swiftly and continues firing. This goes on for five minutes. Snake is feeling better and decides to retreat. He crawls into the hole, where DomeTread entered through the Invisi-Dome. ShaVenger, who is still watching the fight, is the only one who noticed Snake escaping. Z jumps backward, far away from DomeTread and catches his breath.

DOMETREAD. Aw, does little human boy want his mommy? Aw, boo hoo!

AGENT Z, *laughing*. This guy. Heh. (*A Vactra bopper appears in his right hand.*) Time to end this.

The V-Link activates. Z starts running toward DomeTread. DomeTread is getting ready. The V-Link makes multiple copies of

Z. DomeTread and ShaVenger, are surprised. Suddenly, many copies of Z are charging toward DomeTread. DomeTread quickly slams its hammer arms at the ground, and the ground cracks open. Many Z copies fall into the cracks, and DomeTread is cracked in the head from behind. Now only one Z remains, and he has a clear shot. Z blasts DomeTread in the face, and the robot falls on its back.

AGENT Z. I told Caj I would get you. (*The Vactra bopper disappears, and a V-Cuff appears in his hand.*)

DOMETREAD, *speaking gibberish.* Ista lim ba sim Zaban capturain.

Z notices that DomeTread is being teleported and, foolishly, runs toward the robot.

AGENT Z. Nooooo! You're not going anywhere. (*Touches DomeTread just as the robot is about to disappear and is taken to VICE along with it.*)

SHAVENGER, *getting to his feet.* No he didn't! (*Looks shocked.*) Ooooohh. (*Teleports to VICE.*)

Back at VLORs headquarters, in the main control room, Commander Addams is with an operator. They seem to have lost Z's signal and are trying to find it.

COMMANDER ADDAMS, *tapping his headset.* Agent Caj, do you copy?

AGENT CAJ, *via headset.* I'm in the middle of a mission. What's so urgent?

COMMANDER ADDAMS. Agent Z's signal disappeared. Put *whatever* you're doing on hold and report to his last coordinates. I'm having them sent to you right now. Over and out. (*Taps his headset off.*)

AGENT CAJ, *tapping his headset off.* What the hell. Z man, you better be all right. (*Teleports to Z's last known location and looks around.*) Come on, Z. Where are you?

Meanwhile at VICE, ShaVenger teleports near Dr. Machenist's laboratory and walks inside, looking around. Dr. Machenist notices ShaVenger.

DR. MACHENIST. Can I help you?

SHAVENGER. Did a kid around my age appear here with DomeTread?

DR. MACHENIST. DomeTread was alone when he transported in. The kid was not with him.

SHAVENGER, *his words blurting out angrily.* I saw him! (*Becomes hesitant and begins surveying every corner in Mache's lab.*)

DR. MACHENIST, *approaching ShaVenger.* Say the kid did follow DomeTread back to VICE? Just how do you know this? Were you there?

SHAVENGER. No!

DR. MACHENIST. Because if you were there, General Talgitx would definitely have you—

SHAVENGER, *raising his voice.* I said I wasn't there okay! (*Angrily leaves Dr. Mache's laboratory.*)

DR. MACHENIST, *smirks and continues his repairs on DomeTread.*

Z, who's hiding in the ceiling vents, slowly and quietly starts to crawl away from Dr. Mache's laboratory, trying to find a way out. He discovered that he cannot teleport out of VICE. While crawling through the vents in the ceilings, Z tries to contact VLORs using the

V-Link. It's no hope. Z keeps going until he falls down below into a room. He finds himself inside another laboratory. Hearing voices approaching, he hides in a nearby closet. At the same time, ShaVenger is walking down the halls of VICE, angrily talking to himself.

SHAVENGER. I know what I saw. He came here. *He groans.*

GENERAL TALGITX, *walking toward ShaVenger.* Ah, if it isn't Joel. Please do tell. Who came here?

SHAVENGER. No one, sir. (*Standing straight.*) You know me. (*Laughs a little.*) I talk to myself. It's no one.

GENERAL TALGITX. Really?

SHAVENGER, *looking serious.* I wouldn't lie to you, sir …I mean, General.

GENERAL TALGITX. Very well then. Carry on. (*Walks past ShaVenger but turns around.*) Oh and next time you leave VICE without being told to, I will have you punished. Do you understand me, Joel?

SHAVENGER, *whispering.* Shit. (*Answers Talgitx.*) Yes, General! It won't happen again.

GENERAL TALGITX, *turning around again and walking away from Joel.* We wouldn't want to have to summon your stepfather up here.

SHAVENGER. Yeah, wouldn't want that. Pfft. (*Walks away.*)

Z is hiding in a closet when a scientist enters the laboratory. Through the cracks in the closet, Z sees a figure wearing full robes of some sort. It's like the man is trying to conceal who he really is. Another scientist, DR. Machenist, enters the laboratory. The two discuss something new for VICE—something that will change everything. Z starts to think that, maybe, if he gets closer to a window, he'll be able to teleport out of VICE. He notices that the scientists appear to be searching for something. The full-robed scientist near the closet is about to touch it when Z bursts out, knocking the scientist to the floor. In the process, the man's robes unravel, revealing his true self. Dr. Mache looks at the other scientist in shock. Z goes into shock as well when he sees the alien. He quickly leaps back into the vent and crawls through it, looking for an exit. Z materializes his blaster and shoots ahead of him. He sees the sky ahead and teleports out.

AGENT CAJ, *now standing in the spot Z was last traceable by VLORs from.* Come on, Z man.

AGENT Z, *teleporting through the air and then falling on the ground, where he looks around wildly, his face terrified, as if he's just seen a ghost.* Aliens. Aliens at VICE. Alien scientists.

AGENT CAJ. *He runs over to help Z get to his feet and trying to calm him down.* It's okay! Z! It's okay; you're safe.

AGENT Z, *breathing in and out slowly and becoming calm.*

AGENT CAJ. Let's get back to VLORs, Z.

Z and Caj teleport to VLORs headquarters. Back at VICE, Dr. Mache is looking at his former mentor, and for the first time he sees clearly the face of the thing that was under all those robes.

DOC KRARN, *getting off the floor and dusting himself off and hiding the fact that he's pissed.* I guess my cover is blown.

DR. MACHENIST. You're a … You're an alien. (*Is clearly astounded.*) Aliens do exist. Oh my god. This is amazing.

DOC KRARN. Yes we do. (*Walks over to a metallic closet.*) You may leave now, doctor.

DR. MACHENIST. No. Are you kidding me? (*Takes out a taser-blade.*) There's so much I've been waiting to know. I must know about how extraterrestrials compare to humans.

DOC KRARN. I'm afraid you will continue to wait.

Attempting to taser his former mentor, Dr. Machenist slowly eases toward Doc Krarn. Doc Krarn unlocks the metallic closet, and another alien steps out.

VULKARN, *stepping out of the metallic closet.* What can I help you with, my maker?

DR. MACHENIST. No way. You created a copy of yourself. Fascinating specimen.

DOC KRARN. Doctor, please excuse yourself.

DR. MACHENIST. Oh no, my former mentor. (*Smiling at this discovery.*)

DOC KRARN, *nodding to Vulkarn.* Do it.

Vulkarn nods back and walks toward Dr. Mache. Dr. Mache tries to defend himself, but Vulkarn pushes him hard against the wall. Dr. Mache pushes the emergency button, alerting all of VICE, just before slipping into unconsciousness. VICE grunts head toward Doc Krarn's office. Doc Krarn and Vulkarn take their leave from VICE, fighting their way through VICE grunts, making their way to the transport room, and then teleporting out. General Talgitx and several VICE grunts make it to the teleporting room too late. General Talgitx becomes even more infuriated with his VICE grunts, which he's progressively seeing as pathetic excuses for soldiers. They always fail. Instead of sending out a search party for Doc Krarn, Talgitx decides to forget about the alien. He immediately gets a team of scientists together to complete the ongoing project. Billions of metallic bodies and billions of electronic emitters have been made and will go into the final production phase.

GENERAL TALGITX. The statistabots will be born.

Season 1, Episode 4

Wednesday, May 24, 2107

A week and a half later, Zadarion is leaving his last class for the day. After receiving a call from VLORs while at his locker, Zadarion speeds out of Centransdale High School. He finds a place to transform into his agent gear and heads to Flavrare County, IL, where there was a rumored breakout at Gowdon's Prison. Z had placed a few inmates in there recently. Upon arrival, he explores the area, making his way to Lexus Street near a wide-open field. He is followed by three ex-cons who broke out of Gowdon's Prison, who are sneaking behind him, hiding behind large objects. Z hears a noise but doesn't turn around and instead keeps walking but more slowly, intentionally dropping tiny grenade pellets on the ground. One ex-con steps on one of the pellets and slips, hitting his head on the concrete and being knocked unconscious. There was a tiny explosion but it did no real damage. Z turns around and welcomes the other escapees.

AGENT Z. Well, well, well. (*Smirks.*) What's the matter? Food didn't taste too good in lockup?

The escapees attack Z, and he fights them off. After three minutes, the remaining two escapees are on the ground and unconscious. A voice calls Z's name, taunting him.

THE VOICE. Excellent, my young warrior. But you're not done yet.

A total of thirty other escapees from Gowdon's prison all come out of hiding. Z gets ready. The thirty escapees surround Z. It takes Z a full twenty minutes to beat all the escapees and to immobilize them with V-Cuffs. Z is somewhat out of breath. The voice becomes furious, and its owner decides to reveal himself. A tentacle-armed alien emerges from an underground elevator that rises to the surface. Z is confused. The voice reveals who he is and how he and Z met in the past. The voice belongs to none other than Doc Krarn. Doc Krarn has been plotting to kill Z; unfortunately, the thirty-three escapees from Gowdon's prison failed at their assigned task. Doc Krarn reveals his secret weapon—Vulkarn teleports next to Doc Krarn.

DOC KRARN. For years, I have been on Earth. It took some snot-nosed little brat to discover my identity. I have been here since the year 1999. How dare you blow my cover?

AGENT Z. So you been hiding on Earth for years in a doctor's disguise, and you're mad at me?

DOC KRARN. Oh, you will feel my wrath. (*Signals Vulkarn to attack.*) Make a mess of him if you desire.

AGENT Z, *getting in his fighting stance.* Don't get even madder when I destroy your creation.

Vulkarn charges at Z and swings his fist from above. Z jumps back and kicks forward. Vulkarn slaps Z's foot down and swings his foot. Z catches Vulkarn's foot. Z pounces off the ground and charges at Vulkarn. He materializes his blaster and fires multiple shots at Vulkarn, who raises his arm to avoid getting hit. Z throws a punch, and Vulkarn wildly punches back. After a while of heavy fighting, Z surprisingly gets the upper hand and lands an uppercut, following it with a swift kick to Vulkarn's stomach and then smacking his blaster across Vulkarn's face. Z jumps back. Vulkarn growls and then charges at Z. Z jumps high, but Vulkarn grabs Z's foot. Z blasts Vulkarn's hand and then uses his other foot and kicks Vulkarn across his face. Vulkarn face-plants on the ground. Z summons the Vactra boppers and then slams his fist down on the ground next to where Vulkarn is laying. Vulkarn pounces up and grabs Z's head, but Z swiftly backflips over Vulkarn and then swings his right Vactra bopper into Vulkarn's abdomen. Vulkarn gasps for air. Z punches Vulkarn again, this time in the face. Z lands another uppercut, lifting Vulkarn a little off the ground and sending him to the ground on his back. Doc Krarn howls out in anger. Vulkarn growls angrily, and Z swings the Vactra boppers at him again, this time smacking it across the right side of his face. Vulkarn is getting pummeled, and Z appears to enjoy delivering the pummeling. It's as if something is being born inside of him. Z stops his attack and looks at Vulkarn, who is lying on the ground with his arms spread out. Z, exhausted now, looks at Doc Krarn. He's breathing heavily and looking a little devious, but that look vanishes from his face in a few seconds.

AGENT Z. Well? (*Breathing heavily.*)

DOC KRARN, *looking down at Vulkarn. He is upset that Vulkarn is not strong enough to take care of Agent Z.*

Vulkarn rises up slowly. Z takes out his blaster. Vulkarn has trouble looking up but eventually manages to look into Z's eyes. Doc Krarn shoots Vulkarn from behind with one of his tentacles that is laced with toxic venom. Vulkarn disintegrates and is nothing more than a slimy, oozing liquid. Z starts breathing rapidly. He's never seen anyone die before and looks terrified but manages to keep his guard up.

DOC KRARN. If you want something done, then you gotta do it yourself. (*Takes a few steps forward.*)

AGENT Z, *gulping.* Oh yeah. I'll beat you down too!

DOC KRARN. Not in your condition, human child. (*Spreads his many arms and legs out, ready to attack.*)

Doc Krarn makes his way toward an exhausted Z. Z stands up straight, preparing for what might be his last fight. Z starts hearing ticking. Bombs go off, and Doc Krarn is blasted a few feet back. Doc Krarn growls and looks up. Z's eyes go wide. Doc Krarn growls angrily at Z, but the attack wasn't the work of Z. Doc Krarn shoots toxic venom at Z repeatedly. Z dodges by rolling on the ground multiple times. There's a venom shot heading his way, and a deflector shield appears in front of him. An agent becomes uncloaked and is standing in front of Z.

AGENT Z. Rahz? (*Stands up.*)

DOC KRARN, *roaring in pain.* Stupid human! Stop moving!

Doc Krarn is being distracted by a quick-moving Caj, who appeared so fast that no one saw him arrive. Caj is using ninja techniques and dodging Doc Krarn's toxic attacks, all the while landing successful punches. Rahz lowers her deflector shield and raises her blaster. Z stands from his crouching position and takes out his sword.

AGENT Z. You know, I didn't need any help.

AGENT RAHZ, *glares at Z and turning to view the fight between Caj and Doc Krarn.*

Doc Krarn has had enough and lets out a loud roar. He swings all his arms at once, and they smack into Caj, knocking him against a pole. Agents Rahz and Z spring into action and charge at Doc Krarn. Z flies up high, and Rahz stays on the ground, shooting her blaster at Doc Krarn while dodging his attacks.

DOC KRARN. Looks like I'll just have to kill two more. *Swings his many arms at Rahz and Z, who is up in the air trying to land an aerial attack.*

AGENT Z. Stop moving! *Trying to find Doc Krarn's blind spot.*

AGENT RAHZ, *remains mute while steadily dodging Doc Krarn's arms.*

AGENT CAJ, *getting back to his feet.* Hey! *Shouts at Doc Krarn.* Eyes on me, freak!

DOC KRARN, *growls.*

Doc Krarn pulls his arms back, which tricks Z and Rahz. The two are frozen to one spot, looking perplexedly at Doc Krarn. A few arms emerge from underneath Rahz and strike her, but she refuses to fall on the ground and backs away. Distracted, as he's watching Rahz, Z is pulled to the ground by one of Doc Krarn's arms. He attempts to slice at the tentacle around his foot before being smacked against the ground. The tentacle releases Z, who stands back up and gets close to Rahz. Z and Rahz are both ready, and together they wait for Doc Krarn to attack again. Z suggests they form a new plan of attack, but Rahz doesn't hear him, and she charges at Doc Krarn, dodging the tentacle arms by blasting them away. Caj jumps in and slices at Doc Krarn's torso. Doc Krarn becomes angrier and sends one of his tentacle arms to strike Caj, but Caj spins his body to bypass it. Z charges in, shooting his blaster repeatedly, only to be knocked on his butt. A tentacle is heading toward Z, but Caj takes the hit. As Caj begins to suffer from a paralyzing poison, Rahz continues to shoot at Doc Krarn, all the while easily dodging Doc Krarn's tentacles. Z charges in and slices Doc Krarn's torso, launching his foot into the alien's midsection. Doc Krarn falls back. Z and Rahz fall back and stand beside a poisoned Caj. They decide to retreat, but Doc Krarn has a trick up his sleeve. He activates an Invisi-Dome that he created himself, thus preventing the three agents from leaving. Rahz and Z charge in and attack, Rahz is pointing her blasters and firing nonstop. The lasers don't appear to be doing much damage to Doc Krarn's skin. Z appears behind Doc Krarn in the air and holding his sword the wrong way. Z is about to slash Doc Krarn in his back, but Doc Krarn knocks him out of the sky. Z smashes into Rahz. Z and Rahz get off the ground.

AGENT RAHZ, *getting off the ground and dusting herself off.* Stop being so clumsy.

AGENT Z. Sorry. *He gets off the ground.*

The two young agents dodge another tentacle armed with toxic, paralyzing venom.

AGENT Z. *He is scrunching up his face in thought and then turning briefly to Rahz to yell a quick instruction.* Do what you do best! *Flies up high.*

Rahz is confused, but she charges at Doc Krarn and opens fire— clearly not playing around. She distracts Doc Krarn long enough for Z to successfully land an attack. He jumps high and slams his sword at Doc Krarn's head. Doc Krarn knocks Z to the ground and shoots toxic venom at Rahz.

AGENT Z, *getting off the ground and seeing the venom shooting toward Rahz.* No! *Gets in front of Rahz and summons his deflector shield.*

Doc Krarn's attack is blocked; it bounces off the shield and flies right back at Doc Krarn, giving him a taste of his own medicine.

DOC KRARN. *Nooooooo! Is suffering the effects of his own attack.* You stupid, VLORs agents! Mark my words; you will die. I fucking promise you! You hear me! Curse youuuuuu!

Doc Krarn's body shrivels up, and he dies a painful death. Rahz walks beside Z and watches in disgust.

AGENT CAJ, *suffering from the effects of the poison. He is unable to move his body.* I want you guys to burn that body to nothing. Do it!

AGENT Z. Uhh, wait why?

AGENT RAHZ. He doesn't want it to fall into the wrong hands. *Pulls out a flame igniter.*

AGENT Z, *surprised.* Whoaaa! *Mutters to himself.* Didn't think she had one of those.

Rahz and Z pull out their flame igniters, along with two gasoline capsules apiece and burn Doc Krarn's alien body before VICE can get their hands on it and run experiments. After the alien body has been incinerated, Rahz and Z grab Caj, and the trio teleports to VLORs headquarters. Z and Rahz take Caj to the Infirmary Ward. After they've placed Caj on a bed, Rahz walks out. Z runs out after her.

AGENT Z. Wait up! *Stops running and catches up to Rahz.*

AGENT RAHZ, *crosses her arms and looks at Z.*

AGENT Z. I just want to say thanks for the assist. I appreciate it.

AGENT RAHZ. No problem. *Continues while passing Z.* Next time, don't choke. *Walks off.*

Agent Z. What? *His eyes go wide.* Choked? Pfft, whatever. *Smiles and walks in the opposite direction.*

AGENT RAHZ, *turns the hallway corner and smiles a little. Her smile fades away quickly.*

Meanwhile at VICE, Dr. Mache meets with General Talgitx in Talgitx's office.

DR. MACHENIST. You wanted to see me, General?

TALGITX. Yes! I need one of your robots to run a test assignment for me.

DR. MACHENIST. Well sure. However, DomeTread has taken too much damage, and it will take a while to repair him. But I do have another robot that's ready to go online. I mean but hey, why not use Joel?

TALGITX, *as if he did not hear Dr. Mache's last words.* Just be ready on my call.

DR. MACHENIST. No problem, General. *Turns his body and exits Talgitx's office.*

Dr. Machenist leaves Talgitx's office and closes the door. Talgitx receives a holo-message. He opens the link, and his boss, the Informant, as a silhouetted image, becomes visible.

INFORMANT. What is your report on the alien breakout?

TALGITX. Sir, everything's under control. Despite the fact that Doc Krarn deceived VICE, he was ultimately destroyed by VLORs. He was served his justice. I have taken steps to assure this doesn't happen again.

INFORMANT. You see my urgency to call you, Johnathan. I am starting to fall under the impression that maybe this position is too much for you. I hope I am wrong. What is the latest update on this new project I am helping to finance?

TALGITX. The project is being completed today as we speak. You'll see soon enough how I have improved VICE.

INFORMANT. I have faith in you, General. Do not make me have to call again. *Ends the call.*

TALGITX, *sits in his chair and thinks.*

Thursday, May 25, 2107

The next morning, around eight o'clock in the morning, Dr. Machenist is walking with General Talgitx. Dr. Mache is speaking highly of ShaVenger, while Talgitx is looking indifferent.

DR. MACHENIST. Sir, with all respect, Joel has been here for a long time. He was considered to be a VLORs agent once. I think he should test the latest creation.

TALGITX. Children have no place in the field of battle.

DR. MACHENIST. Welcome to the twenty-second century, General.

TALGITX, *stops walking and faces Dr. Mache.* I shall consider your proposal. Now, shall the kid fail, it'll be on your head.

DR. MACHENIST, *laughing.* I see Agent Z isn't failing VLORs, now is he? *Smiling.*

TALGITX, *pointing his finger at Dr. Mache.* This one chance. *Walks away.* My goal is not to turn VICE into a breeding ground for cross-humans.

DR. MACHENIST, *a smile on his face, watches as Talgitx walk away.*

As the alarm clock in Zadarion's room rings out, Zadarion hops out of bed and gets dressed. He grabs his backpack and goes downstairs and into the kitchen, where he gets a snack and makes a funny face at his baby sister.

MRS. HAILIE JONES. Oh, sweetie. I was meaning to tell you that Sam called you yesterday when you were gone. I told him you were at your grandfather's place. It sounds like someone reeeeally wants to talk to you.

ZADARION, *reddening for a moment at hearing his mom tell the lie he told her as a cover, as he was off fighting crime, and then stuffing his mouth with a muffin.* Did he say what he wanted?

MRS. HAILIE JONES. Nope. He said he will talk to you after school the next day. *She goes to wipe the food off baby Kiley's mouth.*

ZADARION, *swallowing the muffin completely and drinking some juice.* Okay, later, Mom. *He leaves for school.*

Zada's freshman year of high school is about to be over. When the long school day comes to an end, Zadarion runs outside to greet Sam Kerry. Zada and Sam decide to walk home together.

SAM KERRY. Brother, where you been at, man? I called you twice yesterday and missed you at lunch hour today.

ZADARION, *thinks about telling Sam about his extracurricular activities but knows he can't.* I was at my grandpa's house. Sorry, brother.

SAM KERRY. Oh no problem.

ZADARION. My mom said you had something super important to tell me.

SAM KERRY, *bursting out the words.* Oh right! (*Chuckles.*) Almost forgot.

Sam and Zada have been walking down Tarainound Street, passing many convenience stores and restaurants. Before Sam can say anything more, Zadarion falls into a dark circle that appeared underneath his feet. Sam turns around, and seeing no one, starts to think that Zada has abandoned him. He sighs and walks home alone.

Meanwhile, Zada is falling through a dark portal of some kind, from which he falls from the sky and lands in the middle of Drekal Park, located in Hidendale Springs, IL. Zada quickly transforms into his agent gear and throws out an Invisi-Dome.

AGENT Z, *looking around and seeing no one.* Come on! (*Yells loudly.*) Show yourself! Why you bring me here?

Something behind Z pushes him onto the ground. He gets to his feet and looks around—and sees nothing. A voice laughs at him. Z is starting to get pissed off.

SHAVENGER, *appearing out of nowhere and walking toward Z.* Hello, Hello, Hello. (*Smiles.*)

AGENT Z, *turning around to face ShaVenger, his expression angry and his tone demanding.* Why you bring me here!?

SHAVENGER. Damn! Chill would you.

AGENT Z, *materializing his blaster.* I'm not going to ask again.

SHAVENGER, *smiling.* I was wondering when this would begin. *Vanishes in a purple liquid and, appearing behind Z. He wraps his arms around Z's neck.* Gotcha!

AGENT Z, *struggling to break free and dropping his blaster.* Let me go!

SHAVENGER. Let's go for a ride.

ShaVenger attempts to teleport Z and himself but finds he is unable to leave the park because of the Invisi-Dome. Z managed to put up a second before his attempt. ShaVenger appears on top of the park's fountain and drops Z, who glides, using the devices in his boots, and safely lands on the ground. ShaVenger laughs and teleports again. He grabs Z's jacket collar and uses his strength to throw Z a few feet away. Z manages to catch himself and prevent himself from falling.

AGENT Z, *standing up straight*. Some strength.

SHAVENGER, I know right? (*Grins*.) Check this out. (*Stands his ground and waits*.)

Z stands ready. ShaVenger rushes at Z, his speed incredible, and punches Z in his left cheek. Z falls on the ground but rolls ten feet away. He gets to his feet, but ShaVenger sweeps his legs, and he face-plants on the grass.

SHAVENGER, *laughing hysterically*. Need help? *Extends his hand to Z.*

Z spits out grass. He hesitates for two seconds before he jabs his fist into ShaVenger's left kneecap. ShaVenger yells out, grabs his knee, and teleports. Z gets to his feet and looks around.

AGENT Z. I dare you to try that again. (*Looks around*.) Wherever you are.

SHAVENGER, *at the top of the park's restroom facility*. Whatcha lookin' at, dude? (*Smiles and winks*.)

Z glances up at ShaVenger and starts to taunt him. ShaVenger smiles and teleports. ShaVenger appears on Z's left, and Z quickly elbows him in the side, grabs his arm, and uses his strength to throw ShaVenger a few feet away. ShaVenger falls on the ground and slowly gets to his feet, smiling. ShaVenger and Z walk toward each other. When the two are face-to-face, about five feet away, they stop, eyeing each other. Z's expression is serious, and he clenches his fists. ShaVenger is smiling.

SHAVENGER, *still smiling*. How's your friend, Sammy?

Z gives ShaVenger a right straight punch to the face. ShaVenger raises his left arm to block Z's punch. Z ducks low and tries to sweep ShaVenger's legs out from under him. ShaVenger does a backflip. Z punches forward, and ShaVenger grabs his arm. Z uses his other arm and punches ShaVenger in the stomach. ShaVenger lets go of Z's arm and backs away.

SHAVENGER, *cracking his knuckles*. No more Mr. Nice Guy.

The two charge at each other, each throwing a punch, both of which hit their mark. They both send another punch, and the two make contact again. For two minutes, ShaVenger and Z repeatedly throw punches at each other. Then Z jumps back. ShaVenger leaps and dives at Z. Z leans forward and grabs ShaVenger's hands, pulling him down. Z does a roundhouse kick, but ShaVenger catches Z's foot. Z elbows ShaVenger in the back. Z quickly turns his body, and ShaVenger does the same. ShaVenger turns his whole body into a dark shadow and throws a punch at Z. Z ducks low to dodge. ShaVenger slams his foot onto Z, who is on the ground, but Z rolls away from ShaVenger. Z gets to his feet. ShaVenger throws a punch, and his arm literally stretches to go toward Z. Z runs, the arm following him. Z stops and turns around. He materializes his sword and swings it at the extending arm. ShaVenger pulls his arm back.

AGENT Z, *looking completely shocked*. How did you do that?

SHAVENGER, *smiling*. Oh, you liked that! *Laughs and then raises his leg and swings it at Z.*

ShaVenger's leg stretches, aiming itself at Z. Z stays still for a moment. Then he swiftly materializes his blaster and shoots ShaVenger's leg. ShaVenger's leg recoils to its normal size, and he flinches at the searing pain. Z smiles.

SHAVENGER. Laugh at this.

ShaVenger's body returns to its normal state. He is no longer a shadow. ShaVenger raises his right arm and shows that he also has a V-Link. ShaVenger swipes an area on his V-Link. A jet flies into the Invisi-Dome, heading in their direction. Z looks up and gets ready. The jet releases circular, metallic objects, which extend their arms and legs. They look like electricity-controlling robots. The robots line up in front of ShaVenger, facing Z.

SHAVENGER. A gift to you and your VLORs companions. The statistabots. This is for making VICE grunts look foolish. Commander Talgitx was absolutely *fed up* with their failures and had these created. *Speaks to the statistabots.* Try not to finish him too quickly. *Teleports on top of the restroom facility to watch Z battle the statistabots.*

The statistabots begin to swarm Z, and he is blasted back. He gets to his feet, only to be blasted onto the ground again. He is knocked to the ground again and again. After five minutes of getting knocked on his butt and listening to ShaVenger laughing at him in the distance, Z becomes aggravated and materializes his sword again. A statistabot flies at Z, and Z swings his sword at it. The statistabot falls to the ground, but immediately flies back into the air. Z comes up with a strategy. The statistabots fly toward Z, having received a command from ShaVenger to finish him. Z dodges each electric attack and then stands his ground and waits. A statistabot flies at him. Z jumps up high and struggles to slice the statistabot in half. ShaVenger gasps. Z deals with other statistabots similarly before ShaVenger calls them back. Z is standing with his sword and ready to battle ShaVenger again. ShaVenger teleports near Z, and the two do battle. Z swings his sword at ShaVenger, and ShaVenger avoids the blow. ShaVenger grabs Z's right wrist and swipes an area on Z's V-Link. The Invisi-Dome fades away and ShaVenger teleports away from the area, and so do the statistabots.

AGENT Z, *looking at his V-Link.* How did he know? *Quickly teleports to VLORs headquarters before anyone notices him in his agent gear.*

Arriving at VICE, ShaVenger heads to the main control room and finds Talgitx talking to Dr. Mache.

DR. MACHENIST, *a smile on his face*. Well, how was your first assignment?

SHAVENGER. It could've gone better. (*Looks at Talgitx.*) Yo, General, what's the deal? I thought you said the statistabots had impenetrable body armor? This was a failure.

DR. MACHENIST, *placing his hand on ShaVenger's shoulder*. Shhhhhhhh.

TALGITX, *looking first at Dr. Mache and then at ShaVenger*. The assignment given to you was a success. The statistabots tired out Agent Z.

SHAVENGER. He may have been a little tired after I left, but I thought the point of the robots was that they couldn't be beaten?

DR. MACHENIST. They served their purpose and passed the test. We wanted to see if they could handle themselves better in a fight than humans can. And they did. To this day, no more VICE grunts will be sent into fights with VLORs.

TALGITX, *nodding*. Precisely the point, Dr. Machenist. (*Looks at ShaVenger.*) I am also surprised how well your performance went out there. At this point I am considering making you an active agent of VICE.

DR. MACHENIST, *blurting out his words*. He accepts, sir!

SHAVENGER, *clearly beyond surprised, stands frozen in place*.

TALGITX. Very well then.

Suddenly, the doors to the main control room opens up, and a VICE grunt runs into the room. General Talgitx looks at the grunt in disgust. Just as the grunt alerts them of a threat, the sirens go off all over VICE headquarters. A robotic voice comes over the intercom system, "Entry room has been compromised. Entry room has been compromised." Talgitx, Dr. Mache, and ShaVenger immediately head to the entry room. They enter and see a young girl with vines coming out of her head. ShaVenger gets ready to attack, but Dr. Mache stops him. A man moves from the other side of the room to stand at the girl's side.

TALGITX. Ah, well if it isn't Cameron Casey. I see you finally returned to VICE. (*Looks at the young girl in disgust.*) And you brought the other cross-human back.

CAMERON CASEY. Indeed I did. Eraine was out for training. She's ready to assist VICE and to deliver revenge on the person who kidnapped her father. I believe he is a member of VLORs.

TALGITX, *looks as though Mr. Casey just told a lie. He nods, indicating to Dr. Mache and ShaVenger that they leave them alone.*

ShaVenger and Dr. Mache go there separate ways, heading down different hallways.

Meanwhile, in the entry room, Cameron Casey whispers to Eraine, also known as Floral, to go to her room. Floral leaves and heads to her quarters. Talgitx and Cameron Casey walk to Talgitx's office.

TALGITX, *shaking his head.* An agent of VLORs kidnapped Matthew Delpro've?

CAMERON CASEY, *looking directly in Talgitx's eyes.* Do you wish to tell Erai—I mean Floral—that VICE was actually responsible for the disappearance of her father?

TALGITX, *his expression and tone angry.* I was not the one to order Mr. Matthew's capture. You know that!

CAMERON CASEY. Indeed I do. You and I both know who was behind his disappearance.

Talgitx and Cameron Casey nod in agreement.

CAMERON CASEY. Despite your dislike of cross-humans, I see you decided to take an interest in young Joel Rodriguez. *He lets out a short derisive laugh.* The VICE grunts performance got on your last nerves, didn't it?

TALGITX, *with a look on his face that answers Mr. Casey's question.* But is she one hundred percent dedicated to VICE?

CAMERON CASEY, *nodding.* Just try her out.

TALGITX. So let me see if I understand this correctly. (*Pauses for a few seconds.*) It took you three months to get Eraine, I mean Floral, the necessary training to master her gift?

CAMERON CASEY, *sighing.* As you already know, I was having some VICE grunts spar with Floral. I needed her to get the gist of what it's like to be in a fight. I knew VICE grunts weren't the strongest. I left VICE Sunday, February 12, 2107, because the Informant called me about a martial arts instructor who can teach Eraine Delpro've the necessary skills.

TALGITX. So, I am guessing you know the real identity of our boss, The Informant?

CAMERON CASEY. I don't know. I mean, whoever this Informant is, he wasn't lying about this martial arts instructor. To be honest, he was good. But the guy was loony.

TALGITX, *walking over to the window in his office.* I have a hard time believing you, Mr. Casey. (*Turns to face Mr. Casey.*) After you left on Sunday, February 12, 2107, I had my secretary do a background check. It wasn't necessary because you're an escaped fugitive from the NiLum Jail, located in NieCross City, North Carolina. (*Takes a deep breath.*) Unfortunately, that is all my secretary could find about you; other information has been sealed. Now is there anything you care to elaborate on?

CAMERON CASEY, *standing up and looking directly in Talgitx's eyes.* With all due respect, General, what I have told you regarding Eraine Delpro've is one hundred percent accurate. The facts about my life are none of your concern. Please do me the favor and stop digging.

TALGITX, *stares into Mr. Casey's eyes for a while and then lowers his head and smiles a little.* As you wish.

CAMERON CASEY, *walking to the door.* If you need to get in touch with me, you know how to contact me. *Walks out of Talgitx's office, and the doors shut behind him.*

TALGITX, *walking to his wine collection.* Heh. *Smiles, shakes his head, and then pours himself a glass.*

Meanwhile, Floral makes her way to her assigned room. She is walking down a hallway when ShaVenger comes out of hiding. Floral stops, and ShaVenger steps out in front of her.

SHAVENGER, *smiling.* I see VICE had another cross-human. So let me guess? You control plants?

FLORAL, *walks up to him and looks directly into his eyes.* Watch it, shadow-stalker. (*Looks him up and down.*) I mean, unless you want to wake up next to poison ivy. (*Smiles.*) Toodles! (*Walks past ShaVenger and continues down the hall.*)

SHAVENGER. Heh, *his smile turning to a frown.* I'll be watching you, Floral. (*Teleports to his assigned room.*)

At VLORs, Z walks into the main control room and sees Rahz, Caj, and many service operators. Commander Addams has everyone line up single file, facing him.

COMMANDER ADDAMS. It has come to my attention, well *our* attention, that our enemy, VICE, was harboring an alien aboard the VICE vessel. Thanks to the absurd actions of a fellow agent, the alien became a wanted man. VICE had put out a bounty on one of its own—scientist Doc Krarn, who, according to a fellow agent, was on this planet since the year 1999. *He lowers his head and sighs.* The threat of him has been neutralized, thanks to three of our agents... *He points to Z, Rahz, and Caj.* You guys. *He looks at everyone.* This puts something new into the mix. Aliens, new armored statistabots, cross-humans, and who knows what else may be thrown at us. But let us not forget our main goal—to bring VICE to an end and to protect this world in secrecy. (*Nods to each agent and operator, signaling that the meeting is over.*)

AGENT Z, *walking toward Commander Addams.* Excuse me, sir. That kid I fought was a cross-human? What's that?

Agent Caj, *stepping closer to Addams and Z.* Humans who have come in contact with chemicals or radiation of some kind and have mutated as a result.

COMMANDER ADDAMS, *nodding at Caj.* That's correct, Caj. *Looks at Z and glances up at Rahz.* The kid was Joel Rodriguez. He used to be one of us.

AGENT CAJ. He started a little after I did. The year 2103, I believe.

AGENT Z. That explains why he deflected all of my moves. He is well trained—almost like us.

AGENT CAJ, *joking.* You sure it wasn't just you, Z man? (*Has a smile on his face.*)

AGENT RAHZ, *giggles but controls herself.*

AGENT Z, *turning and looks at Rahz and then grimacing at Caj.* No, it was not me!

AGENT CAJ. I'm kidding, Z man. (*Looking at Addams.*) My apologies, sir.

COMMANDER ADDAMS. Joel came to VLORs around the same time as Caj. Joel was eleven years old then. Upon the time of his swear-in, to become an official VLORs agent, Joel went MIA. Reports came back that Joel was moved to another location in the city. I believe he was taken hostage by VICE and has been brainwashed for four years.

AGENT Z. He didn't seem to be brainwashed.

AGENT CAJ. Oh and don't forget, sir. Joel wasn't a cross-human when he was here at VLORs. VICE had to have done experiments on him.

AGENT RAHZ, *taking a step forward.* Excuse me for interrupting, Commander. But are there any special strategies we can do to immobilize these ...cross-humans? I'm assuming the V-Cuffs wouldn't work on them.

COMMANDER ADDAMS. Oh no, you're fine Rahz. You see the V-Cuffs were modified before you and Z came aboard. We didn't think this necessary, but now, we are grateful that the scientists who invented VLORs technology thought ahead.

Commander Addams leaves the room. The operators sit at their stations again, monitoring areas for any unusual activity. Caj leaves the room and walks down the hallway opposite the one Addams took. Rahz leaves the room next and heads for the escalator. Z watches her as she walks away and remembers Sam Kerry. He races down the hallway, making his way to the Geared'NReady room. From there, he teleports out of VLORs and appears just outside of his house in an alleyway. Instead of going home, Z runs to Sam's house. Making his way closer to Sam's house, Z sees a moving truck. He ignores the truck and knocks on the door. Sam opens the door.

SAM KERRY, *not looking too happy.* Oh, hey.

ZADARION. Hey, brother. What's up? (*Panting.*) Sorry about earlier. You see, I remembered I had to pick up something for my moms at the store. I know I should've asked you to come along. But look, I'm sorry, brother. So what's with the movers taking things out of your house?

SAM KERRY. I'm moving.

ZADARION. WHAT?!

SAM KERRY. Yeah. Mom got reassigned to another position at her job. They need her somewhere else.

ZADARION. Nooo! (*Looks at all the boxes being loaded on the truck.*) So this is what you wanted to tell me?

SAM KERRY, *leaning on the side of the door.* Yup. I just didn't think you cared anymore.

ZADARION, *looking surprised by Sam's answer.* What do you mean, Sammy? We're *best* friends.

SAM KERRY. Lately you've been avoiding me. I know. I know what you said, but still.

ZADARION, *grabbing Sam's shoulders.* There's gotta be something we can do. Let's go talk to your mom.

SAM KERRY, *gently removing Zada's arms.* I tried, brother.

ZADARION. No, no, no! This isn't fair! (*Stomps his foot.*)

Sam's mom tells the boys to take a walk down the block so Zadarion can cool off. The two walk side by side.

ZADARION, *walking with both hands in his pockets.* So, where you moving to?

SAM KERRY. Varilin Capitol in New York.

ZADARION, *shaking his head and then turning to face Sam.* I'm sorry I made you feel like I was neglecting you. (*Tears come to his eyes.*)

SAM KERRY, *facing Zada.* It's okay. But, dude, not the waterworks. (*Is unable to stop his eyes from watering too.*)

Sam Kerry and Ryan "Zada" Jones share a meaningful hug. The two walk shoulder to shoulder, their arms around each other's backs to Sam's house. Sam's mom calls Sam's name, telling him to hurry up. Sam turns to face his best friend in the whole wide world.

ZADARION. *He chuckles.* You're like the only person, besides my parents, who knows my real name is actually Ryan.

SAM KERRY. *He smiles.* A combination of your nickname and real name your parents gave you.

ZADARION. Yeah. *He sniffs.* This isn't good-bye though. Not by a long shot. *He holds out his hand.* We'll see each other again.

SAM KERRY. Is that a promise? (*He shakes Zada's hand.*)

ZADARION. Damn straight. (*Smiles.*)

SAM KERRY. Hell yeah. (*Smiles back.*)

Zadarion and Sam laugh because Sam's mother did not hear Zada and Sam swear. The two friends share one final hug. Sam runs to his mom's car, and Zada watches as they drive off into the sunset. Zadarion stands on the curb for what feels like hours until he finally walks home. Zadarion walks into his house, looking upset.

MRS. HAILIE JONES, *noticing Zada's sad expression.* Oh my. You and Sam said your good-byes, didn't you?

KILEY, *uttering her first words.* Zadie! Zadie!

ZADARION, *bawls and runs upstairs.*

KILEY, *expecting Zada to give her a funny face, looks at her mother, expressionless.*

MRS. HAILIE JONES. *She is hurt that her son lost his best friend but she knows that he needs some time alone right now. She says quietly to herself.* It will be all right. You and Sam will see each other real soon.

Zadarion enters his room and falls on his bed, crying into his pillow. After an hour, Zadarion takes a quick shower and goes to bed. At the same time, somewhere just near the Illinois state border, during the car ride, Sam Kerry cries himself to sleep.

Meanwhile, Floral/Eraine is in her room at VICE, sitting with her legs crossed on her bed, looking at a picture of her father she placed on her nightstand.

FLORAL, *talking to the picture.* I wish you could see me now, Daddy. I've become stronger. I'm not going to die now. Your cure saved me. You see, Daddy? *Takes a deep breath.* I'm not mutating into a monstrosity after all. Don't you see me, Daddy? *Her eyes begin to water. She picks up the picture frame and lies on her side, tears in her eyes. She hugs the picture of her dad close to her heart.* Can't you see me, Daddy?

Eraine was born with a disease that was genetically passed down from her mother. When Eraine was eight years old, her father, Matthew Delpro've, created a cure and gave it to his daughter. It took awhile before her body showed any improvement. Several weeks later,

Eraine's genetic structure started rebuilding itself. Unfortunately, the cure had a side effect Mr. Delpro've couldn't have predicted. Eraine gained an ability called Chlorokinesis—plant control. Eraine became a cross-human. Mr. Delpro've took Eraine to VICE while he worked on a cure. Mr. Delpro've was frightened and had dreams about his sweet little Eraine mutating into a monstrosity.

Two events led to Mr. Delpro've worries. The first incident was that Eraine was caught communicating with flowers in her bedroom. The second incident was when, a few days after Eraine was cured from her illness, Mr. Delpro've was attacked by a thug, and Eraine mysteriously summoned a vine to stop the thug from beating her father, leaving the thug hospitalized. Mr. Delpro've's research was interrupted when a member of VICE found out about Eraine. Mr. Delpro've went missing. To Eraine's knowledge, her father was captured by VLORs. Eraine has built a hatred for VLORs—thanks to Mr. Delpro've's old friend.

When an old ally of VICE, Cameron Casey, returned to Hidendale Springs, IL., Mr. Casey encountered his old friend's daughter. Mr. Casey befriended Eraine and got her to accept her gift. She was recruited into VICE. Mr. Casey trained Eraine, and then the Informant ordered him to have her train with someone else. On Sunday, February 12, 2107, Mr. Casey took Eraine to meet with a skilled but loony martial arts master. While away from VICE, Mr. Casey explained everything about her father's research to Eraine. He told Eraine that a member of VLORs had captured Matthew Delpro've and had taken him to a secluded location. Mr. Casey told Eraine that she had the option of being normal again, telling her that he ordered VICE scientists to find a cure for her condition. Eraine denied help. She did not want to be cured. She wanted to find the person who had captured her father. Eraine wanted revenge. Mr. Casey helped Eraine to become stronger. Eraine soon called herself, Floral.

FLORAL, *wipes her eyes, still holding the picture frame close to her chest and falls asleep.*

Season 1, Episode 5

Friday, May 26, 2107

After lunch hour at school, Zadarion receives an incoming holo-message from Commander Addams. He throws away his garbage, grabs his book bag, and exits the cafeteria. He walks into a restroom stall and locks the door and then activates his V-Link and opens the holo-message. The message instructs him to head down to Valora Docks in Valousse City, IL. Zada transforms into his agent gear and teleports to Valora Docks. Once there, he cautiously approaches one of the boat housing warehouses. From the other side of the wall, he listens in on three individuals. He uses his V-Link to activate his scope lens, which allows him to see through the wall and discover there are four individuals, not three.

CLOUDIS MONROE. I don't know about this plan of yours, man. We already disbanded once. We're reduced to a few members.

DOMOS. That's the point, man. (*Standing in the center of the group.*) Darkstras is locked away in NiLum Jail. He's not getting out ... ever. Many of the old gang have gone into hiding. (*Shakes his head.*) Pfft, cowards. They don't understand that KyrosDOOM will never die.

CLOUDIS MONROE. You want to revive the old gang?

DOMOS. Nah, bro. I want to create a newer team—you, me, and just a few others. (*Nods to the other two people in the room.*)

Agent Z notices one of the men in the group is Ray Gardner, aka Snake. His appearance is human now.

SNAKE, *interrupting Cloudis and Domos.* Look, Darryl, this sounds good and all. But how do ya'll hope to get around them damn VLORs agents? (*Looks at Domos.*)

Domos is about to attack Snake for saying his real name, but Cloudis gets in between them.

CLOUDIS MONROE. Eeeasy, Domos. He's still new.

DOMOS, *growling.* Call me by that name again. I dare you! (*Fixes his shirt and is calm.*)

CLOUDIS MONROE. I have a solution for them VLORs agents. (*Points to the fourth guy in the room.*) My newest friend is a former CIA agent turned criminal. He escaped from Primous Facility. Told me he had to swim across waters and that he hijacked a boat just to get here. Ron Battleton here is an excellent sniper, and he's skilled in hand-to-hand combat.

Agent Z sneaks quietly into the warehouse.

DOMOS. Then they will be our main muscle. (*Points to Snake and Ron.*)

CLOUDIS MONROE. So, Team KyrosDOOM is alive once again.

DOMOS. You missin' the picture completely, son. I said *new* team. We call ourselves KYROS-X.

RON BATTLETON. I like it.

SNAKE. Yeah, that name kills.

CLOUDIS MONROE. Then it's unanimous.

AGENT Z. Ew no. Change the name.

The four members of the newest team of villains, KYROS-X, all look around the warehouse to see where the voice came from. Snake transforms into a snakelike creature, and Ron pulls out his guns. Z is hiding behind a broken computer station. Z uses his blaster and shoots Snake and Ron into different corners of the warehouse. Domos throws a barrel at the spot where the shots were fired. Z comes out of hiding and shoots the barrel.

AGENT Z. Yeeeeaahh, I don't think your new team is gonna make it. *He fires his blaster at Domos.*

Cloudis Monroe surprises Z and kicks his blaster out of his hand. Z starts blocking Cloudis's punches. Cloudis gets kicked in the chest and hits the floor. Ron sprints on foot toward Z and starts shooting his guns. Snake pounces off the ground, swinging on the ceiling's rafters, aiming at Z. Z summons his deflector shield to block the bullets fired from Ron's gun. Ron is now in close range, and he swings his left fist at Z. Snake lands on the ground, missing his attack. Snake and Ron are dueling Z. Domos is pacing back and forth, watching the fight, waiting for his opportunity to attack. When Ron runs out of bullets, Z punches him in the face and back kicks Snake. Z grabs Ron's left arm and swings him around, slamming him into Snake. Domos and Cloudis charge at Z together. Domos swings his fist, and Cloudis swings his leg. Z catches Cloudis's foot and pulls Cloudis in to take Domos's punch. Cloudis gets knocked on the ground, and Z jumps high and knees Domos in his jaw. Snake jumps back in, and Z grabs his blaster from off the ground and smacks it into Snake's face.

AGENT Z. This is fun and all, but I'm gonna be late for class.

Ron sneaks up behind Z and grabs him from behind, lifting him up off the ground. Z bashes the back of his head into Ron's face. Ron's grip loosens. Z turns around and punches Ron in the chest as hard as he can. Ron gasps for air, and Z roundhouse kicks him to the floor. Snake charges once again, and Z shoots a paralyzing shot at him.

Snake evades the hit. Cloudis yells to the team to retreat. Domos runs in and fights Z. The two are going blow for blow. Cloudis helps Ron onto his feet, and the two make their way to the roof. Snake wraps his tail around Z, and Domos punches him in the chest area. Z gets thrown and smashes into a damaged boat. Domos and Snake follow Cloudis and Ron to the roof, making their way to Cloudis's jet. Z gets to his feet and away from the damaged boat. He hears the jet's engines roar. Z runs to the roof, but he's too late—the jet has already taken off.

AGENT Z. Damn! *He taps the button on his headset and contacts VLORs, asking for Co. Addams.* Agent Z to Commander Addams. My report. Four criminals met together at Valora Docks in Valousse City, IL, to form a new team. They call themselves KYROS-X. They said their former name was Team KyrosDOOM. What I learned is that they have two new members, one of them being a cross-human thug I fought before and the other, a former CIA agent. This gang, team KyrosDOOM, I don't know if they're legit or not. Maybe you guys know about it. Anyway, this concludes my report. I have to get to class. (*Ends the call.*)

Zadarion teleports back to a restroom stall at Centransdale High School. He exits the restroom and makes it on time to his last class of the day.

As Zada exits the restroom, a young boy with black and reddish hair saw him. This boy knew he was the only one in that restroom until Zada left the restroom.

After the last class of the day is over, the boy with black and reddish hair meets Zada at his locker.

ALECXANDER JACKSON. You dropped this leaving the restroom. (*Hands Zada his notebook and walks away.*)

ZADARION. Oh, thanks. (*Realization spreads across his face.*) Wait! He saw me. (*Quickly turns around but does not see Alecxander.*)

Zadarion realizes that his secret identity might have been compromised. He gets a call from VLORs. He positions his right arm inside his locker, and the V-Link appeared. Checking the call, he learns that DomeTread is about to wreak havoc again. The giant robot is heading toward the arcade and restaurants in Hidendale Springs, IL, and he's getting close. Zada grabs all his things and makes his way into town, transforming into his agent gear when he's almost there. He arrives at the scene to see people fleeing past him. A news reporter actually catches a glimpse of him, before tripping and landing on his face. Z throws out an Invisi-Dome. The news reporter forgets why he was running. He, and everyone else around, saw no destruction.

In the Invisi-Dome, Z follows the path of destruction caused by a rampaging DomeTread. But he sees something new. A young boy is flying around DomeTread using electricity powers. Z stands there, watching. DomeTread crashes his way forward until he is a few feet in front of Z. DomeTread is transported back to VICE. Z glances up and made eye contact with the new hero. The new hero runs on foot, attempting to escape, but is unable to get out of the Invisi-Dome. The young boy, who is wearing goggles to hide his identity, looks at Z and then walks toward him.

AGENT Z, *looking confused.* Who are you?

SHOCKER. You can call me Shocker. (*Points behind him.*) You gonna let me out of here?

AGENT Z. I don't know cross-human. Should I?

SHOCKER, *laughing.* This again. (*Stops laughing.*) You gon' try and capture me now, aren't you?

AGENT Z, *materializing his sword and smiling.* It's my job. (*Swings his sword at Shocker.*)

SHOCKER, *jumping back, sparks flying out from his fingertips.* Bet you won't try that again.

Z runs toward Shocker, swinging his sword again. Shocker twirls his body to dodge. Then, facing Z, he shoots lightning sparks at Z. Z brings his sword in front of him. Shocker controls the sparks, causing them to push against Z's sword, trying to push him back, but Z has a firm grip on his sword. Shocker redirects the sparks into the sky above, and they evaporate.

SHOCKER. What's your name?

AGENT Z. Nunya. (*Charges at Shocker.*)

Z swings fiercely and Shocker gracefully dodges. But Z has a trick up his sleeve. Z swings lefts, and Shocker falls for it. Z spins his body quick and kicks Shocker in his side. Shocker jumps backward. This momentary lapse of attention gives Z time to press the release button on his V-Link and then he places his sword on his shoulder, causing the Invisi-Dome to disappear. Shocker tries to leave the area and is successful. Z smiles and quickly teleports to a nearby rooftop.

AGENT Z. He fought well. I won't capture him yet. (*Smiles. His V-Link beeps.*) Hmm? Another activity.

Flashback – The remainder of this episode jumps back in time, following Agent Rahz's initiation to VLORs.

Monday, April 10, 2107

It is fifteen minutes before 1:00 in the afternoon, and school will be over for the day soon. Zhariah is sitting at her desk with her hand under her chin. She is looking at the words that Professor Nakosa had just written on the dry erase board during his philosophy lecture— Logos, Ethos, Pathos. Two girls are sitting in the back of the room, giggling and talking about boys, their nails, and other teenage stuff. Zhariah turns her head and looks at the two girls.

MARIE MIKAELSON, *rolling her eyes*. Ugh. What are you staring at, loser?

DELANA BLOOME, *flashing a wide, irritating smile*. Loooser!

ZHARIAH, *turns to face the dry-erase board again.*

As the bell rings throughout Centransdale High School, students flood the halls, heading to their lockers and out of the building. Zhariah closes her locker and turns around, only to be shoved aside by Marie Mikaelson.

MARIE MIKAELSON. Out of the way, loser.

DELANA BLOOME. Yeah! With your out-of-date clothes. Who you buy from—Cheap-O'Mart. (*Laughs.*)

Marie joins her friend in laughing. Zhariah would love so much to wail on the girls, but as usual, she doesn't bring herself to do it. Holding in her tears, she picks up her belongings and exits the school. Zhariah walks down Tarainound Street to get home. She lives on Himswelm Street, right across from Narthaniel Park District. Zhariah lives at Abigail's Home for Youth Foster Care—an orphanage that does not receive appropriate government funds. The funds the facility has suffice, but it could use more. The owner, provider, and mother figure is Abigail Johnson. Abigail "Auntie-Mama" is a widow who raises the children housed at the home as if they were her own. Auntie-Mama is a heavyset, middle-aged woman with a big heart. Abigail does what she can to get food, clothing, and supplies from other resources. A total of ten children, ages five through seventeen, live in the foster home.

Zhariah makes it home and drops her belongings in a room she shares with two others—a girl who is a know-it-all and little Maya Johnson. Maya Johnson is Zhariah's non-biological little sister.

ZHARIAH, *places her bag and books on her bed and sighs.*

MAYA JOHNSON, *being chased, runs behind Zari.* Zari, Zari … Save me, save me!

ZHARIAH, *crossing her arms.* What have I told you boys?

CAIL AND ADAM, *speaking in unison.* But she took our—

MAYA JOHNSON, *protesting loudly.* I didn't take anything!

ZHARIAH, *looking at Maya then at the two boys.* Just get outta here.

CAIL AND ADAM. *They walk out of Zari's room, pouting.*

ADAM. *Continues pouting.* Always take her side.

Zhariah and Maya walk down the hall to the kitchen.

MAYA JOHNSON, *seeing Michel.* Hey, Michel! *Runs to Michel and hugs him.*

ZHARIAH, *stopping and watching.* What's up, bro?

MICHEL JOHNSON. *He plays with Maya's hair.*

MAYA JOHNSON. *She giggles.*

MICHEL JOHNSON, *looking at Zhariah.* You had a good day at school?

ZHARIAH. Yeah. But you know, Auntie-Mama gon' be mad 'cuz you weren't there.

MICHEL JOHNSON. Shhhh. (*Smiles.*) She doesn't have to know. (*Winks and walks away.*)

ZHARIAH. Going out again, huh?

MICHEL JOHNSON. Yup! (*Walks out the door.*) Later.

Zari and Maya walk into the kitchen, and Maya sits at the table. Auntie-Mama is preparing dinner for the foster children. Auntie-Mama notices Zari's expression.

AUNTIE-MAMA. You okay, sweetie?

ZHARIAH, *in another world.* Huh! Oh yeah, I'm good.

AUNTIE-MAMA, *loading a big dish into the oven.* That's nice.

MAYA JOHNSON. Can you take me to the park, Mama?

AUNTIE-MAMA. Oh no, I'm sorry dea—

ZHARIAH. I'll take her!

AUNTIE-MAMA, *smiling.* Be home on time.

ZHARIAH. We will. Promise.

Zhariah takes Maya, Cail, and Adam to Narthaniel Park. Maya brings her toy ball along with her. After thirty minutes of playing, a mean kid throws Maya's ball into the street and runs off. Maya cries out. Zhariah hears Maya and goes to see what's wrong. Maya points at the boy and explains what happened. Cail and Adam return with Maya's ball, and Zhariah watches the little boy. Becoming furious, Zari goes after him. She chased the boy across the street and into an alley, where she corners the boy and is about to fight him. The boy backs against the brick wall and cowers, his hands over his head.

ZHARIAH, *rolling her eyes.* Little wuss. Don't do it again.

The boy runs past Zari, yelling. Zari realizes she left Maya, Cail, and Adam at the park alone. Zari knows she'll be in trouble, especially if Auntie-Mama can see that Maya has been crying. (For some odd reason, Auntie-Mama knows all.) Zari runs back to the park and walks the three little ones back home to the foster home. Unbeknownst to Zari, Agent Caj, who had been cloaked, was standing on the ledge of a building, staring down into the alley and was watching her the whole time.

AGENT CAJ, *laughing.* Ohhh …this one is going to be a keeper. (*Teleports away.*)

Zari and the little ones have arrived home from the park, and dinner is being served. It's now 4:00 in the evening. When everyone finishes eating, the older ones go to their rooms, and the younger ones head off to the play area. Zari goes outside and climbs onto the roof. This is her thinking spot. After ten minutes, she half dozes off. In her half-awake state, she envisions the orphanage being destroyed. She jerks herself awake and sits up straight. She feels something in her hand and looks down to discover that she is holding a mysterious device. Caj placed the V-Link in her hand while she was daydreaming. The device teleports Zari to VLORs.

Zhariah sees nothing but white lights. She notices she is still holding the device and looks around, trying to figure out what happened. Zari spots a young man leaning on the wall in front of her. He smiles and walks up to her.

AGENT CAJ. I'm Agent Caj. I've been watching you. You're a potential.

ZHARIAH, *feeling weirded out.* You been watching me?

AGENT CAJ. Nah, nah. *Laughs and holds his arms out in front of him, palms up.* Just recently in that alley. Follow me.

ZHARIAH, *following him warily.* Are you going to like arrest me or something? I didn't hit him. (*Is worried.*)

AGENT CAJ, *keeping his eyes forward.* In my opinion you should've. Kid had it coming. (*Stops and points.*)

ZHARIAH, *reading the sign he's pointing to.* The Center. (*Looks confused.*) What's in there?

AGENT CAJ. All right; short version. I am a special task force agent. This is VLORs, a highly advanced secret organization. We're dedicated to world peace. My commander wanted you brought here. You've been selected. This room, the Center, is like the gateway to a whole new world for you. If you wish, we'll enter. If you decline, you'll have your memory erased, and you will not remember what I have just said—or being here. (*Leans on the wall next to the door.*) So, what's your answer?

ZHARIAH. You kidding me, right? (*Looks at the ground.*) I'm not good at anything though. (*Looks up at Caj.*) Why choose me? I'm incompetent. It's what people at school say.

AGENT CAJ. Do you really believe that?

ZHARIAH, *hesitates for a minute and then decides.* Yes! I want to be an agent.

AGENT CAJ, *winking at Zhariah.* Awesome. (*Opens the door and points into the room.*) After you, young lady.

Zhariah steps inside the room, and Caj walks in behind her. Angela greets them both.

AGENT CAJ, *leaning on Angela's desk.* A new agent for you to process, Angela.

ANGELA RUNN. Oh excellent. (*Looks at Zhariah.*) Hi!

ZHARIAH, *appearing nervous.* Hi. *Waves and then places her hand back at her side.*

ANGELA RUNN, *typing on her computer.* Please go stand behind the line.

ZHARIAH. Okay. (*Walks over to the spot.*)

ANGELA RUNN. No need to be shy. This is just the oath of enlistment.

The automatic door to the office shuts, and a monitor drops down in front of Zhariah. The monitor turns itself on, and none other than Head Commander Addams's face appears on the screen.

VOICE. Please state your name.

ZHARIAH, *standing up straight.* My name is Zhariah Johnson.

VOICE. Thank you. Please repeat what you see on the screen. Begin!

ZHARIAH, *taking a deep breath.* I, Zhariah Johnson, do solemnly swear to support and defend the VLORs agency against all enemies, foreign, domestic, or alien; that I will bear true faith and allegiance; and that I will obey the orders of the head commander of this here agency of VLORs and the orders of the higher agents appointed over me. So help me, I will remain faithful to this cause until the bitter end or have my full memory erased permanently. (*Sighs.*)

AGENT CAJ, *makes a funny face.* Here it comes.

A machine lowers down. A needle comes from the machine and collects a blood sample.

ZHARIAH. Ow!

The machine returns to where it came from.

AGENT CAJ, *laughing a little.* I didn't like that part either. It's just necessary.

ZHARIAH, *rubbing her now bandaged arm.* What's next?

Angela Runn presents the paperwork, and Zhariah signs it agreeing that it seems pretty understandable, even the memory erasing part. Caj explains the training to her, urging her to hurry, as she only has two hours before she needs to get home, and then deposits her at the training room.

AGENT CAJ. Later, Z girl. *He leaves the room, waiting out in the hallway.*

Zhariah walks into the room and meets the training droid that will be instructing her through the training.

PHYSICAL READINESS DROID. Hello and welcome to physical training regimen. Today's training will be a simulation of an actual mission. You will be given the tools to deliver an outstanding performance. However, how you choose to use the tools depends on you. Each person has a unique style. If you step to your right, we will begin by setting you up with the training arsenal.

ZHARIAH, *walking to the spot the droid indicated and standing still.* Okay?

A transparent circular tube comes out of nowhere and encloses itself around Zhariah. Zhariah's clothing is replaced by a tight, white, fitted T-shirt and baggy, white cargo pants. Her shoes have been replaced with all-black combat boots. A metallic silver belt with a black, box-shaped belt buckle wraps around Zhariah's waist. Zhariah's curly hair wraps into a bun, giving her a new hairstyle. Finally, as white gloves cover both of her hands, the device Caj placed in Zhariah's hand emerges from her pocket and wraps around her right wrist.

The transparent tube opens up, and Zhariah walks out. She is totally impressed.

AGENT RAHZ. So wicked!

PHYSICAL READINESS DROID, *gliding across the room and coming to a stop in front of Rahz.* Whenever you feel ready, please stand completely motionless and repeat these words: "Simulation begin." (*Glides to a corner.*)

AGENT RAHZ, *watching the droid position itself in a corner and then takes a deep breath.* Simula— Hold up. (*Thinks.*) I think I better see what I can figure out first. *Looks at her wrist and fiddles with the device. The V-Link activates, and she locates the information she needs. The V-Link tells her about all the devices at her disposal.* Okay, I'm pretty sure I'm ready. (*Takes a deep breath.*) Simulation begin.

The surroundings change shape, and Rahz is now standing on the side of a gas station. Rahz peeks out and sees two drug dealers transacting a sale. Rahz watches carefully and then materializes her blaster.

The drug lords are hard-looking criminals. Drug Lord 1 is wearing a leather jacket with a symbol of a snake on the back, and drug lord 2 has on a jean jacket with rips on each side. Rahz decides to hide behind the broken-down car nearby. She ducks low and slowly makes her way to the car.

DRUG LORD 1. So this is what I got … Take it or leave it.

DRUG LORD 2, *appearing to be wasting time.* All right. Deal. (*Pulls out the cash to pay.*)

DRUG LORD 1. You hear that? (*Looks over at the car and sees a foot sticking out.*) Behind the car, idiot!

DRUG LORD 2, *pulls out his gun.*

AGENT RAHZ, *quickly raises her body over the car and shoots the two drug lords in the chest.*

Rahz dives back behind the car, thinking she missed her targets. The simulation ends, and the droid glides to Rahz.

PHYSICAL READINESS DROID. Score of 94 out of 100. No displays of sarcasm, effective. Analysis occurred. Subject would have been more successful if legs weren't shown while hiding. A second simulation is needed in order to pass level. When ready, repeat the words, "Simulation begin." (*Glides back to the corner.*)

AGENT RAHZ. What! But I passed.

AGENT CAJ, *walking into the room after hearing her score.* Whoa! That's awesome.

AGENT RAHZ. No it isn't. I have to retest. This is some—

AGENT CAJ. Whoa, potty-mouth! (*Laughs.*)

AGENT RAHZ. Uh, not really. I was going to say …this is some crap.

AGENT CAJ, *laughing.* Alright. I'll just be outside the room. (*Leaves the room.*)

AGENT RAHZ, *smiling.* He's a clown. (*Laughs lightly, and then stands ready.*) Simulation begin.

The room once again changes shape. Rahz finds herself hiding in what appears to be a concrete, cylinder tube. She does a quick recon and sees a scientist standing by a computer, armed guards standing by all exits, and a test subject that's being experimented on. Rahz activates her stealth mode. (Her body turns invisible.) She approaches the guards and neutralizes them with V-Cuffs, which activate silently. Rahz walks over to the computer and turns off her stealth mode. The scientist sees her and signals the guards, not realizing they've been neutralized. The scientist looks back at Rahz, who jumps up and kicks him to the floor. Using the control box in his sleeve, the scientist activates the test subject, revealing it to be a robot. Rahz notices the electrical line above the robot's head. Before the robot can stand up, she shoots the line. Massive amounts of electric sparks fill the air, causing the robot to explode. Seeing the computer about to begin its self-destruct mechanism, Rahz goes over to the computer, and her V-Link reboots the system. The simulation ends.

PHYSICAL READINESS DROID, *gliding toward Zhariah.* Score of 98 out of 100. No displays of sarcasm or unnecessary commentary, very effective. Above average analysis occurred. Subject targeted the electrical wires to take out the test subject but did not use them on the guards. Appears to have taken into consideration the whole laboratory catching fire. Use of physical agility is well above average, and firing skills are superb. Second simulation accessed and passed. Until next time. (*Glides back to the corner.*)

AGENT RAHZ, *in disbelief.* A 98, huh? Really?

AGENT CAJ, *applauding while entering the room.* Well, I'm impressed! (*Laughs.*) I wouldn't worry about those two points. It's above average. A perfect score just starting out is …good. (*Walks Rahz out of the room.*) Let me show you around. Walk with me.

Caj takes Rahz to the main floor. They pass the recreational facilities and the cafeteria and then enter the room where agents prep for their missions.

AGENT CAJ. This is the Geared'NReady room. You won't necessarily need to use the other facilities much. I just wanted to show you where everything is located. So, what do you think?

AGENT RAHZ. It's all pretty awesome. *She scrunches up her forehead in thought.*

AGENT CAJ. You got a question?

AGENT RAHZ. Is the food here good? I heard about military food; just wondering.

AGENT CAJ. It'll suffice. (*Laughs.*)

AGENT RAHZ. So when can I expect to go on my first assignment?

AGENT CAJ. Commander Addams will let you know. You got the V-Link, right?

AGENT RAHZ. Yeah. (*Raises her right arm.*)

AGENT CAJ. This is very important. It is what gets you in and out of this place. Your V-Link is a device capable of transforming you into your agent gear. Each one is unique to each agent here at VLORs. You remember the blood sample taken from you?

AGENT RAHZ. Unfortunately.

AGENT CAJ. This has that uniqueness that is encoded within your DNA structure. The device teleports your body, meaning it disintegrates your body into tiny particles from any location and finally to the VLORs base.

AGENT RAHZ. Well, what if it malfunctions and I have no way of contacting VLORs? How can I get here?

AGENT CAJ. Good question. There's a link embedded into the V-Link that automatically repairs itself. The scientists here at VLORs run maintenance checks while an individual is wearing one. (*Sighs.*) Also, no one even knows where VLORs is located. I heard it's constantly moving. That may be a lie.

AGENT RAHZ. It's too bad I cannot finish my training today. I have to get home.

AGENT CAJ. Mhm.

AGENT RAHZ. I promise I will be back as soon as possible to finish. So, how do I use the teleporting feature?

AGENT CAJ. Just think it. When the V-Link is strapped to your wrist, it's connected to your nervous system. Focus and think about your home or VLORs, and presto, you're there. Try not to tell anyone about today too. (*Extends his left hand to shake hands with Rahz.*)

AGENT RAHZ, *shaking Caj's hand.* Well, thanks, Caj. I'll be seeing you. (*Concentrates on where she lives and teleports home.*)

Commander Addams comes around the corner and sees Caj.

COMMANDER ADDAMS. Ah, just the man I was looking for.

AGENT CAJ. Yes, sir. What can I do for you?

COMMANDER ADDAMS. There's another kid I need you to go find. He lives in Hidendale Springs, IL. So you don't have to travel far.

AGENT CAJ, *laughing.* Another one.

The two go down different hallways.

Meanwhile, Zhariah has successfully teleported onto the roof of her home. She hears Auntie-Momma shouting her name and goes to find her.

ZHARIAH. I'm right here, Auntie-Momma. You need something?

Auntie-Momma. Time for bed.

Zhariah. Oh right. Sorry. (*Laughs a little.*)

Zhariah goes into her room and notices her roommates, Maya and Michelle, are fast asleep. Zhariah goes into the bathroom; takes a quick, cold shower; and gets into her pajamas. She lays on her head down and goes to sleep.

Monday, April 17, 2107

A whole week has past. Rahz passed weapons training with flying colors. She has been given a few missions, involving drug busts and other secret assignments. VLORs trainer Tim McGraw took an interest in Rahz's high score in weapons training and has taken her under his wing for more advanced training in military grade weaponry. Rahz has showed some real growth this past week. Currently, Zhariah is at Centransdale High School.

While Zhariah is in school, two bank robbers are on the run from Dowers City police officers. According to the officer's report, the robbers have their faces covered and are armed. Officers surrounded the Dowers National Bank building, ordering the robbers to come out. A group of officers smoked their way into the bank, and the two bank robbers made their way to the roof of the bank, followed by the police. The two men were cornered on the rooftop, but the bigger one fought the officers, injuring them. The bank robbers jumped from rooftop to rooftop, eventually making it to the ground. The chase lasted for hours, and the robbers finally made their way through the forest and to the Dowers City Chemical Plant. The police were still in pursuit. A security guard at the chemical plant noticed two masked men and opened fire. When the smaller robber was shot in the leg and then caught a bullet in the side of his arm, he dropped his gun and fell down. The big guy shot the security guard, severely injuring him and then helped his smaller partner, dragging him into the chemical plant. The robbers made their way through the plant but unknowingly walked in and out of an active testing room. As they snuck out the back door, the bigger robber stashed his injured partner behind a tree and returned shortly with a beat-up getaway car. The big guy helped the little guy into the car, and they drove off. The police made it to the spot too late.

After school, Zhariah receives a holo-message instructing her to go to the chemical plant to investigate. Rahz finds bloodstains, but the blood is worthless. Rahz's V-Link senses ammonia. VLORs concludes that the robbers sprayed the substance to avoid having their identities recovered. This is a dead end.

Tuesday, April 18, 2107

The two bank robbers are hiding out an apartment complex called Iron Row, located in Kale, County, IL, where they are renting a room. The two men, Darius Helms (the smaller of the two) and Pesto've Daggerton (the big guy) are unmasked. They are brothers. Darius has fully recovered from his wounds; no bullet wounds are on his body. Darius and Pesto've think this is a miracle, not thinking about the fact that they escaped through the chemical plant.

Wednesday, April 19, 2107

Pesto've and his little brother, Darius, rob Iris's Fashion Jewelry Store, in Flavrare County, IL. The Dowers City Police Department has informed Flavrare County sheriffs about the two robbers they are seeking. Four sheriff's deputies are waiting outside for the two robbers (both police forces are still in the dark about the robbers' identities). Pesto've and Darius (both masked) get into a scuffle with the four sheriffs. While Pesto've fights two of the deputies, Darius is having a little trouble with the other two. Darius has his arm around one of the deputy's necks, but the other is pointing a gun at Darius, ordering him to surrender and to let the deputy go or he'll shoot. A shot is fired and strikes Darius's shoulder. Darius moans and punches the deputy in his spine. Darius then pushed the deputy to the ground. Pesto've surprises the deputy who shot his little brother, tackling him from behind. Another sheriff's deputy uses the opportunity to sneak up behind Darius. He smacks Darius in the back of the head with his gun. Darius gets up quickly and slams his fist as hard as he can into the deputy's face. The deputy hits the ground and is out cold, with a burn mark across his face. Darius sees fire disappearing from his hand. Pesto've gives his brother an odd look before slamming the other cop on the ground. The four deputies are unconscious, and Pesto've and Darius both run.

Later that night, Darius tries explaining to his brother that he doesn't know what happened back there. Pesto've doesn't question Darius.

Thursday, April 20, 2107

Pesto've and Darius are walking down Lexus Street in Flavrare County, IL. Just as the two pass the wide-open field and Mackie's Donuts, four sheriff's deputies stop their cars next to them. The pair fits the description of the Dowers City bank robbers and the perps from Iris's Fashion Jewelry Store in Flavrare County perfectly. Pesto've feels a burning sensation and smiles deviously. He charges in and unleashes a handful of fire at two of the deputies. Then, laughing, he blasts fire at the other two.

DARIUS HELMS, *running up next to Pesto've and slapping his shoulder.* What the hell? You too?

PESTO'VE DAGGERTON, *laughing.* Come on, brother. Let's show these cops.

Darius pauses and looks at his brother. The deputies are hiding behind their cars as Pesto've shoots fire at them. While Pesto've is busy playing with the deputies, a lone deputy is hiding at the side of a nearby building. The officer fires a bullet at Pesto've. Darius sees this and shoots fire from his hands. The bullet heading for Pesto've is incinerated. Pesto've stops his attack and looks at his brother. He growls at the officer and blasts fire at him. Two deputies are injured, and the others are struggling to stand.

DARIUS HELMS. Brother, we gotta get out of here!

PESTO'VE DAGGERTON, *laughing.* What's the rush? *Laughs even louder while his hands ignite with flames.*

A light flickers in the sky above Pesto've and Darius's heads (an Invisi-Dome activates). The two robbers look to the sky. There is a brief silence.

DARIUS HELMS. What the hell? (*Looks around and sees a young girl walking toward them.*)

PESTO'VE DAGGERTON, *laughing.* Jailbait. (*The flames on his hands are getting bigger.*) Heeere, kitty, kitty. (*Blasts fire at the approaching girl.*) Buuuuuuurrrnnnn, baby Buuuuuuurrrnnnn!

The girl jumps up high, as if she's flying in the air. A shocked expression crosses Darius's face, and Pesto've growls and lifts his arms high, fire still shooting from his hands. The girl is gliding with the wind, avoiding the flames. Suddenly, she disappears.

PESTO'VE DAGGERTON, *stops shooting fire and looks around.* Where'd you go?

DARIUS HELMS. *Yelling.* Behind you!

Darius lifts his left hand and shoots fire but misses the target. The girl appears in front of Pesto've's face and kicks him in the chest. Pesto've falls on his back. The girl falls to one knee and looks at Darius, who screams and shoots fire. The girl rolls on her side and throws tiny daggers at Darius, missing her mark for the most part, perhaps intentionally. One of the tiny daggers barely strikes Darius's shoulder, leaving a cut. Pesto've gets off the ground and shoots fire at the girl. The girl gets to her feet and flips backward, dodging the fire. Pesto've continues shooting fire. The girl is about thirty feet away now, hiding behind a shield. Darius walks to his brother's side and watches the fire striking the shield.

PESTO'VE DAGGERTON. Only a matter a time, brother. Then we're outta here. (*Chuckles.*)

Darius sees a light and turns his body around slightly. By the time he realizes he's looking at a tiny explosive device (a Q3 explosive), it's too late to act. The bomb goes off and knocks Pesto've and Darius on the ground. The girl stands up, and the shield disappears. Darius is on his hands and knees and hears nothing but silence. The girl walks closer to the two robbers. Pesto've attempts to get to his feet, but the girl kicks him in his side, lifting him two inches off the ground before he falls back down. Angry, Darius gets mad and jumps to his feet. Still unable to hear anything, he takes a swing at the girl. The girl moves to the side and then punches him in the face. Darius falls back to his knees. He sees a metal object appear in the girl's right hand. Pesto've roars and grabs the girl from behind, squeezing his arms tightly around her chest. The girl struggles to break free from Pesto've's massive arms.

PESTO'VE DAGGERTON. *Screaming at his brother.* Darius. Stand up! (*Squeezing tighter.*) Finish her!

Darius stands up and regains his hearing a little. Breathing heavily, he looks at the girl. She stares back at Darius with fury in her eyes.

PESTO'VE DAGGERTON. Hurry, brother! Kill her!

Darius, *still breathing heavily*. All right.

Darius punches the girl several times. She stops struggling and, eventually, stops moving at all. Darius and Pesto've thinks she's dead. But just when Pesto've loosens his grip around her, she quickly wraps her legs around Darius's neck, pulling him closer. Darius is choking and can't get free. Pesto've tightens his grip, but the more he does, the more the girl tightens her grip around Darius's neck. Pesto've drops the girl on the ground, and Darius falls on the ground too. She releases her legs from around Darius's neck. Pesto've grabs his little brother and takes off running—and smacks into an invisible wall.

Agent Rahz, *getting to her feet*. Going somewhere? (*Looks at the two of them.*)

Pesto've Daggerton, *growling*. Put down this invisible wall. *Now*!

Agent Rahz, *raising her right arm and then getting into a fighting stance*. Come make me.

Pesto've Daggerton, *growling and letting go of Darius's shirt collar. Let's out an infuriated roar and charges at the girl.*

Rahz stands her ground. When Pesto've is within five inches of Rahz, he finds himself in a chokehold. Rahz has Pesto've's left arm and neck trapped in her arms, and her right leg is closed around his right arm. Rahz quickly releases her grip on him and jabs her fist at his neck. He falls to the ground, inadvertently grazing the device on Rahz's right arm on his way down, which releases the Invisi-Dome. Rahz looks over at Darius, and a V-Cuff appears in her right hand. Pesto've laughs, and Rahz looks at him.

Pesto've Daggerton. *He lets out a maniacal laugh and coughs a few times*. Stupid girl.

AGENT RAHZ, *looking back toward Darius and seeing no one.* Where'd he go? *She raises her voice.* Tell me!

PESTO'VE DAGGERTON. Gone. *Continues laughing and starts coughing.*

AGENT RAHZ. Ugh. *Tosses the V-Cuff at Pesto've, and once he's immobilized, contacts VLORs.* Agent Rahz to Commander Addams. I captured one hotheaded robber, but the other escaped. Don't worry. I'll find him. This I promise. Agent Rahz out.

Thanks to the V-Cuff, Pesto've was teleported to Gowdon's Prison in Flavrare Town, Illinois. That evening, a discreet Darius targets local jails in order to get his brother out of jail. Disguised as a security guard, Darius goes to Gowdon's Prison and he breaks his brother out overnight.

Meanwhile, Zhariah settles in her bed and goes to sleep.

Season 1, Episode 6

Monday, May 1, 2107

As morning comes, Zhariah rises from bed, feeling her best. She takes a shower, gets dressed, has a quick snack, and heads to school. The morning pretty much follows the same routine as always for Zhariah. At school, Marie Mikaelson and Delana Bloome continue to be their ignorant selves, making fun of Zhariah's hand-me-downs and social status. Zhariah does her best to ignore them. At lunchtime, all the students head to the cafeteria.

Meanwhile in College Station, Texas, the CEO of Stratum Oil, Dale Falakar Jr., is leaving a business meeting. Dale Jr. leaves the office and enters one of his laboratories, walking by many hardworking scientists. An employee bumps into him.

STRATUM OIL EMPLOYEE. Oh my apologies. Forgive me.

DALE JR. It's fine. (*Smiles and straightens his jacket.*) We aren't taking a quick break now, are we? (*Looks the employee sternly in the eyes.*)

STRATUM OIL EMPLOYEE. No, sir. I was just collecting today's files to log into the system.

DALE JR. Ah. Carry on. (*Watches as the employee walks back to his workstation.*)

Dale Jr. receives a phone call on his cell. He walks into the hall and answers it.

DALE JR. Dale Falakar speaking.

UNKNOWN CALLER. I hope you did not forget our meeting arrangement?

DALE JR. I was just about to give you a call. I'm on my way. (*Ends the call and makes his way to the elevator.*)

Dale Jr. leaves the laboratory and drives to Port Aransas, Texas.

Meanwhile, in Hidendale Springs, IL, the students at Centransdale High School are just now leaving lunch hour. Zhariah makes her way to free period. Her V-Link activates, and she goes into the girl's restroom to answer the call.

COMMANDER ADDAMS. Ah, Rahz. How is school going?

ZHARIAH. It could be better. What do you need from me, sir?

COMMANDER ADDAMS. I need you in College Station, Texas, immediately. I'm sending the information now.

ZHARIAH. Lucky for you, I have free period. (Peeks out of the restroom stall.) I'll be there. (*Transforms into her agent gear and teleports to the coordinates sent to her V-Link.*)

Dale Jr. arrives at the warehouse located in Port Aransas, TX, and walks inside. A slim young man with blond hair is standing near some computer equipment. Dale Jr. approaches the young man, who greets him with a smile. The two shake hands.

DALE JR. I see you're doing well, Mr. Mathessen. How's your work at Vale Corp in Melovaton City, South Carolina?

ANDREW MATHESSEN, *sighing.* It's going well. Did you bring the stuff?

DALE JR. *snaps his fingers, and his bodyguard and driver enters the warehouse and stands next to him, holding a briefcase.*

ANDREW MATHESSEN, *eyes widening and smiling equally as wide.* Yes! (*Takes out his money card to pay.*)

DALE JR. You sure are running out fast.

ANDREW MATHESSEN. What can I say? I like to travel.

DALE JR. That's one reason I developed something new. (*Steps in front of the briefcase and opens it.*)

ANDREW MATHESSEN. *Gasping.* What did you do?! *His smile fades away.*

DALE JR. Relax, child. (*Turns his body and faces Andrew, holding a small capsule.*)

ANDREW MATHESSEN. *He starts to get angry. His raises his voice.* This isn't what we agreed!

DALE JR., *calmly.* Relax and listen.

ANDREW MATHESSEN, I swear if you try to scam me—

DALE JR. Oh, this isn't a scam. More like ...the future.

ANDREW MATHESSEN, *is quiet.*

DALE JR., *holding the small capsule.* I've noticed how my other brand wasn't lasting very long. I thought about an endless supply of oil. SupeXoil has been modified to last longer than your usual dosage. (*Points to Andrew's backpack.*) I know you use SupeXoil to fuel that contraption on your back. (*Remains quiet for a while.*) I would love to see what it is you invented for yourself. (*Smiles.*)

ANDREW MATHESSEN. I know you would. (*Looks serious.*) So this special oil blend will last ...how long?"

DALE JR. About six monthS before your next ...recharge. (*Places the capsule back into the briefcase.*) Might I suggest a nonexplosive method? My scientists have completed the SupeXelectric capsules.

ANDREW MATHESSEN. Thanks, but I'm fine for now. (*Scans his money card on Dale's money transfer device.*)

DALE JR. Transaction completed. (*Smiles and hands Andrew the briefcase.*) Pleasure doing business with you again.

ANDREW MATHESSEN. Uh-huh.

Andrew takes one of the capsules out of the briefcase and takes off his backpack. The backpack opens up, and Andrew takes out an old capsule and replaces it with a new one. The backpack loads up his flight device.

DALE JR., *admiring Andrew's flight device.* Fascinating. (*Smiles.*) Why not come work for me?

ANDREW MATHESSEN. Thanks, but no thanks.

DALE JR., *frowning a little.* Too bad.

ANDREW MATHESSEN. Yup! (*Places the backpack on his back.*) See ya later, Falakar. (*Flies out of the warehouse at an incredible speed.*)

Dale Jr. and his bodyguard leave the warehouse. They get inside the car and drive off. Rahz, who is watching from on top of the warehouse throws a tracker device onto Dale Jr.'s car. The tracker scans the entire car and everything inside. Rahz calls Commander Addams.

AGENT RAHZ. Commander Addams, this is Agent Rahz. It seemed pretty normal to me. Falakar was selling some capsules to a blond-haired guy. The guy's name is Andrew Mathessen. Should I go after him?

COMMANDER ADDAMS. Negative, Rahz. With the tracker in place, we can monitor all of Falakar's activities. For now, go back to school.

AGENT RAHZ. Okay, sir. (*Teleports back to school.*)

Rahz arrives in the girl's restroom, where her V-Link disappears, and she is transformed back into her civilian clothes. Zhariah listens outside the restroom's stall for any noises. After ascertaining that the room's deserted, she steps out into the hall.

Wednesday, May 10, 2107

The school day has ended, and Zhariah is at her locker. Sam Kerry and Zadarion are leaving the building. Marie Mikaelson pokes Zhariah. When Zhariah turns around, she acts like she didn't do anything. Zhariah tightens her fists as Marie and Delana Bloome walk away. Zhariah turns back around, facing her locker, and closes it. She walks out of the school building. She's walking down Tarainound Street when her V-Link activates. She enters an alley and answers the call.

COMMANDER ADDAMS. Pyro and Dyro are out and about again. They are in Dowers City, Illinois.

ZHARIAH. Dyro must've freed his partner in crime somehow. Don't worry, I will make sure they both are arrested and thrown away in jail for good.

Zhariah hides behind a dumpster and transforms into her agent gear and then teleports to Dowers City. Rahz is standing at the top of Dale's Shopping Center building. She looks around but sees no one. Then suddenly, she spots the two walking near the forest and teleports there.

PESTO'VE DAGGERTON. We did good this time. (*Admires the jewels they stole.*)

DARIUS HELMS. Let's just get back to Mom's. (*Walks rapidly.*) Before she shows up again.

PESTO'VE DAGGERTON. Yeah, Mom could use us by her bedside right now. *Looks angry.* But when I see that little girl aga— *Dodges a dagger that was thrown at him.*

AGENT RAHZ, *catching the dagger as it spins back into her hand.* I'm sorry. What was that?

DARIUS HELMS. Shit. *Turns and looks at the girl standing behind them.*

PESTO'VE DAGGERTON. Take these Dyro. *He growls and charges at Rahz, howling in rage.*

DARIUS HELMS. What? No, Pyro! *Sighs.* Damn! *Leaves the area.*

Pesto've slams his flaming fists at Rahz. She flips backward, and her boots kick Pesto've in his jaw. Pesto've backs away a little, but he ignites his hands again and charges at her. Rahz dodges each flaming punch and punches him in the face. Pesto've growls and blasts fire at her. Rahz materializes her deflector shield just in time. The flames stop, and when Rahz lowers the deflector shield, she sees no one. Pesto've, for the first time ever, has retreated from a fight. Rahz activates an Invisi-Dome, just in case someone witnessed the fight. The Invisi-Dome surrounds the area and then disappears. Rahz teleports around Dowers City, IL, inconspicuously, before heading home for the day.

Friday, May 12, 2107

Arnold McManon (Dr. Machenist) arrives in College Station, Texas, via SpeedWay Rail Station and then travels by cab through the heart of Brazos Valley on his way to Stratum Oil Industries. The cab driver drops him off in front of the parking garage.

ARNOLD MCMANON. Wait outside until I return.

CAB DRIVER. Yeah. All right.

Arnold McManon walks into the first floor of the parking garage located near Stratum Oil Industries. There is a man in the shadows in front of him.

ARNOLD MCMANON, *is looking around the parking garage.*

DALE JR., *approaching Arnold McManon and holding a briefcase.* I don't know why we always have to do this in secrecy.

ARNOLD MCMANON. Trust me. It's best you don't ask. So is that SupeXoil?

DALE JR., *nodding.* And a more improved version.

ARNOLD MCMANON, *shakes his head.* Very nice. *Takes out his money card and scans it on Dale's money transfer device.*

DALE JR., *handing Arnold McManon a briefcase full of capsules.* Another successful transaction.

Arnold McManon grips the briefcase close to him. The parking garage lights start to flicker, and Arnold activates his disgraceful mock V-Link, turns invisible, and leaves Dale Jr. behind. As the light remains steady, Dale Jr. looks at the spot where Arnold McManon had been standing. Seeing no one there, Dale Jr. smiles.

DALE JR. Whoever you are, if you're going to assassinate me, at least do it with style. (*Remains standing, one hand in his pocket.*)

Dale Jr. looks around the parking garage again, and the lights flicker once more. He catches a glimpse of a tiny person before he is grabbed by his suit collar and thrown to a concrete support beam.

DALE JR., *raising himself up.* The strength on you. My God.

AGENT RAHZ, *her face hidden in the shadows.* Falakar.

DALE JR., *trying to get a good look at the person.* Care to show your face?

AGENT RAHZ. Not necessary. (*Kicks him in his chest.*)

DALE JR., *now sitting with his back against the support beam.* Ah. You realize I'm just a feeble old man?

AGENT RAHZ. Shut up. (*Uses her V-Link to scan the area.*)

DALE JR. Sure he's long gone by now. Should've gone after him instead. (*Grins.*)

ZHARIAH, *looking Dale's way and grimaces.* It doesn't matter. My orders were to get *you*!

DALE JR. Whoever you're working with, I don't think my security will appreciate you abducting me.

Dale Jr.'s security team arrives at the parking garage, their guns pointed into the shadows where Rahz is standing. Rahz calmly eyes Dale Jr., not making eye contact with anyone on the security team.

DALE JR., *getting to his feet and smiling.* What are you waiting for… Do it!

Rahz drops a tiny grenade pellet, and when it explodes, she escapes the area. Dale Jr.'s security team runs toward the shadows, but it's too late.

DALE JR., *smiling.* I wonder who's targeting me now?

SECURITY TEAM MEMBER. Sir. Area is clear. You may proceed.

DALE JR. Should've gotten here sooner. (*Smiles and walks away.*)

Having escaped to the rooftop of Stratum Oil Industries, Rahz teleports back home to the orphanage.

Saturday, May 13, 2107

The time is 9:00 in the morning. At Stratum Oil Industries in College Station, TX, Rahz is standing on the roof, cloaked. Dale Jr. is being walked outside to his car by a group of security guards. Dale Jr. has another meeting at Stratum Oil Industries located in Port Aransas, TX (the fourth location that was built). Rahz follows the tracker and teleports to the location. She lands on the roof of the building and makes her way through the vents.

While Rahz is watching Dale Falakar Jr. closely, Pyro and Dyro are chilling at their mom's house in Kale County, IL. Pyro (Pesto've) is looking out the window for cops. Dyro (Darius) is hovering over his sickly mother.

DYRO. This isn't enough for Mom's surgery.

PYRO. Then let's tag another bank.

DYRO, *looking up at his brother.* Yeah and then what? When we get enough money, how are we supposed to seek out a doctor? We're on the news and on the web. They know our faces.

PYRO, *walking over to his brother.* You let me worry about that.

DYRO, *holding his mom's hand*. Yeah. I trust you.

PYRO, *kisses his mom's forehead*. Remember, this is for Mom.

In Port Aransas, TX, at Stratum Oil Industries, Rahz, sitting on the rooftop, is getting bored just waiting. For two hours, Dale Jr. has been in board meetings.

At the end of the board meeting, Dale Jr. walks out of the room, feeling completely irritated. He loosens his tie and, his security in tow, heads down to the parking garage, where he receives a call.

DALE JR., *answering his phone*. Falakar speaking.

UNKNOWN CALLER. Yeah. I heard you got some secret stuff to make engines accelerate faster.

DALE JR. You mean machines?

UNKNOWN CALLER. Yeah, Yeah. I'm going to text you my location. Meet me there with the stuff. I'll bring the money.

DALE JR., *ending the call and smiling*. It looks like I have to grab something from the lab.

SECURITY TEAM MEMBER, *sitting behind the wheel of the car*. Already taken care of, sir.

DALE JR., *looking to his left and seeing the briefcase*. Thank you.

Dale Jr.'s security driver arrives at the warehouse located in Port Aransas, Texas where the text that followed the call directed him. Dale Jr. walks inside the warehouse and sees a young man leaning near the back door. The young man nods at Dale Jr. and indicates he should proceed to the back door. Dale Jr. walks out the back door and approaches two additional men. They all shake hands.

CLOUDIS MONROE. Nice to meet you, Mr. Falakar.

DALE JR. No need to be formal with me. Call me Dale.

CLOUDIS MONROE, *nodding*. Well, all righty then.

DALE JR. I received a call from … (*Points at Domos.*) You?

DOMOS. Yes, sir. *Looks at Dale Jr.* I was told about this special oil you manufactured. How does it work on jets? (*Nods to Cloudis.*) His jet, as a matter of fact.

DALE JR. You will appreciate the speed, my friend. (*Smiles.*)

CLOUDIS MONROE. How much?

DALE JR., *showing a price from his phone*. I'm sure this is reasonable for you.

CLOUDIS MONROE. What does that mean? (*Shakes his head.*) Never mind. Sure. (*Scans his money card on Dale's money transfer device.*) Here you go, Mr. Falakar.

Rahz jumps off the warehouses roof, aiming at Cloudis Monroe and kicking him to the ground. She turns around, only to be kicked in the chest by a newcomer (Ron Battleton). Rahz stands up, facing Ron, who pulls out his guns. Rahz charges at him, and the two duel. Domos pulls Cloudis Monroe off the ground.

DOMOS. *Looking frightened*. Get to the jet and install that thing, Cloudis!

Cloudis Monroe runs to his jet. Domos charges at Rahz, who is dueling Ron Battleton. Domos throws a punch, but Rahz raises her arm to block it. She jumps and kicks Ron Battleton to the ground and then ducks low and punches Domos in his stomach. Dale Jr. is fleeing the scene, running back to his car. Rahz throws a V-Cuff, and it wraps around Dale Jr., immobilizing him. Ron Battleton's fists fly at Rahz, and Rahz barely dodges the onslaught of swift punches. Rahz kicks Ron backward and jumps over Ron's head, missing Domos's kick. Rahz tightens her fists and charges in. She quickly uppercuts Domos and roundhouse kicks Ron. She throws a V-Cuff but the ground beneath her is shot at, and the V-Cuff misses its target. Cloudis's jet is hovering over the group. Rahz dashes for cover. Domos and Ron flee to the jet, and the jet flies away. Rahz looks over at an immobilized Dale Jr.

AGENT RAHZ. Let's see them replenish their supplies with*out* the supplier. (*Contacts VLORs.*) Agent Rahz to Commander Addams. My report. I arrested Dale Falakar Jr. He should be transported in 3 ...2 ...1. (*Ends the call.*)

Dale Jr.'s body is transported to VLORs. He is secretly taken to Gowdon's Prison in Flavrare County, IL. As he's not considered a supercriminal, he avoids Primous Facility.

Rahz teleports to VLORs, arriving in the Geared'NReady room. She makes her way into the main control room to meet Commander Addams.

Someone (most likely one of his employees), from Dale's home state, heard about Dale's imprisonment and went to Illinois to bail him out of prison. Dale was at Gowdon's Prison for only a short time.

Spring 2098—nine years earlier

Two events took place in the year 2085. DiLuAH's ship crash-landed on Earth in Naphilia Town, IL. And miles away in Hidendale Springs, IL, a mysterious knight's tomb cracked open. Now thirteen years later, the mysterious knight crawled out from under Drenden Mountain (located behind Hidendale Observatory). The mysterious knight wandered the strange new world, hoping to find something familiar. He had two goals. The first was to find and kill the witch that had cursed him, and the second was to annihilate the two knight clans, ones responsible for sealing him away. He had no luck. He spent a month, walking on foot, trying to find any clues as to where the knight clans could be hiding. Everything familiar to him had been forever changed. The mysterious knight ended up in Teekee Forest, located near Lamont Town, MI. He heard crying nearby and decided to go check it out.

The mysterious knight walked cautiously. Deep in Teekee Forest, he found a baby boy lying beside two dead bodies and a strange man standing over the sobbing baby. The strange man was playing with his hands, whose fingertips were emitting colorful lights. The strange man heard something coming from behind and teleported away before the mysterious knight's sword could impale him from behind. The mysterious knight sheathed his sword and picked up the baby boy. For some reason, the infant child stopped crying, and the mysterious knight walked off with the baby boy.

Saturday, May 27, 2107

A girl and a boy are walking down Mitchel Street, leaving Kale County, IL, heading to the arcade in Hidendale Springs, IL.

RANI. Oh shoot. (*Stops walking and faces his twin sister.*) I forgot the money Mom gave us.

DANI, *smiling and rolling her eyes.* Relax, bro-bro. I picked it up after you put it down on the kitchen table. You just had to get the last croissant Dad made.

RANI, *sticking his tongue out, teasingly.* Cool. Let's hurry. The quicker we get there, the quicker I can see the tears rolling down your face when I beat— *Heyyy*!?

A shady man wearing a hat and a trench coat has bumped into Rani. Rani and Dani turn and the man keeps walking and then turns around the street corner. Rani chases after him, seeking an apology. But when he turns around the street corner, he sees no one. Dani approaches a bewildered Rani, holding a gadget.

RANI, *still looking but not seeing the shady man, finally turns his head, looking at his sister.* What ya got there, Dani?

DANI. I don't know, but it looks like a gaming console from 1991. I think that man dropped it.

RANI. Oh well. Finder's keepers. Let's hurry to the arcade before it gets dark.

Soon, the twins are at the arcade playing video games.

Meanwhile, a bank robber named Pogo is on the run from Dowers City police officers. A swift force sweeps Pogo away from the area, leaving the police in a confused state.

DOWERS CITY POLICEMAN. Where'd he go?

Pogo smacks into the concrete, right outside of the National Bank on 44th street & Pulaski Avenue. An Invisi-Dome blankets the area around him. Pogo stands up and tries to hop away. Pogo is shot in the chest with a hand blaster. Pogo lands on his back but manages to stand back up.

AGENT Z, *holding out his arm to look at his V-Link and reading Pogo's crimes out loud.* Wanted for aiding and abetting, wanted for selling narcotics to minors, wanted for …hold on? (*Pauses.*)

Oh …and wanted by VICE for selling important intel. (*His screen closes as he lowers his arm.*) So come on; tell me. What secrets of VICE did you sell?

POGO, *speaking in an unidentifiable accent; it definitely sounds foreign.* That's a lie. (*Spits.*) I never stole anything.

AGENT Z, *looking at the ground at Pogo's spit.* Yeah I'm gonna pretend you didn't just spit at me. (*Cracks his knuckles.*) Well, Peter Nigoron …back to Primous Facility you go, buddy.

POGO. *Sounding enraged.* I'm going nowh—

Lightning strikes Pogo in the chest, and he lies on the ground petrified.

AGENT Z. Dude! Come on. Really though?

SHOCKER, *laughing and jumping out of a window.* What? He's all right. I think? (*Smiles.*)

AGENT Z, *smiling a little and pulling out V-Cuffs.* You should get out of here.

SHOCKER. Oh right. Later. *Turns his body into electricity and speeds around the Invisi-Dome.*

As soon as Z slaps the V-Cuffs on Pogo, Pogo is transported to Primous Facility. The Invisi-Dome lifts, and Shocker gets away quickly before VLORs scanners can detect his presence.

Monday, May 29, 2107

The school year is about to end. Zadarion and his school chums have a week before finals. Zadarion walks into Centransdale High School, feeling almost joyful. He is sad that he isn't finishing out the school year with his best friend, Sam Kerry. Zadarion walks to his locker to grab his books. A few minutes later, Kiyla walks through the halls, but something's a little off with her.

KIYLA GERALD, *rubbing her head and not looking up. She bumps into a group of chatty girls.*

GIRL. Uh, excuse you. Watch where you are going with your ugly ass.

KIYLA GERALD, *turning around quickly after hearing the word "ugly".* I know you ain't talking… Usted jirafa alta. *She spoke in Spanish just then.*

GIRL. Girl, uh-uh, *pushing her bag to her friend.* What did you just call me?

JAYLA PRICE, *rushing in between her friend Kiyla and the girl.* Whooooaaa, girl. (*Starts pulling Kiyla away.*) Let's get to class, Kiyla.

GIRL. Nah, leave her alone. Let Miss Prissy get dropped. (*Stands still, ready to fight.*)

KIYLA GERALD, *raising her voice so that everyone in the hall can hear.* Who you calling prissy? *Struggles to get free of her friend's grasp.* Let me go, Jayla.

JAYLA PRICE. You're not yourself right now. (*Continues holding onto Kiyla tightly.*)

PRINCIPAL HARVIEL, *from down the hall, raising his voice.* Ahem. Ladies, do you have somewhere to be?

GIRL, *turning her head to the principal and then back at Kiyla and whispering.* You lucky that ass is looking out for you, freshman. (*Walks away with her group.*)

As the group of girls leave the hall, Principal Harviel continues watching Kiyla and Jayla from a distance. Zadarion is watching from his locker. Jayla pulls Kiyla into the girl's restroom.

JAYLA PRICE. *Explodes once they are alone.* Have you lost your mind?

KIYLA GERALD. No! Have you lost yours? (*Looks in the mirror and then gets in Jayla's face.*) Why'd you interfere? I would've knocked her straight.

JAYLA PRICE. First back up out my face, Kiyla. (*Exhales.*) This is sooo not you right now. (*Paces back and forth and then looks at Kiyla.*)

KIYLA GERALD. What are you looking at? You got a problem with me too? What?

JAYLA PRICE, *exhaling loudly.* I knew we shouldn't have gone to that party. *Faces Kiyla, trying to look in her eyes.*

KIYLA GERALD. *Explosively.* Get out my face! (*Sighs.*) Damn, you're weird. (*Leaves the restroom in a hurry.*)

JAYLA PRICE. Kiyla, wait up? (*Picks up her and Kiyla's backpacks and leaves the restroom, bumping into Zadarion in the hallway.*)

ZADARION. My bad, Jayla. (*Looks worried.*) I saw Kiyla's outburst earlier. Are you two okay?

JAYA PRICE, *blowing air out of her mouth.* You bug, Zada. Would you give me some space. Dang! (*Walks past Zadarion, feeling annoyed.*)

ZADARION. What did I do? (*Leaves to go to class.*)

After a few hours, it is time for the second lunch hour. Zadarion leaves his locker, heading downstairs and entering the lunchroom. Zadarion goes to the line to order food, while looking for Jayla and

Kiyla. Standing in line, he eventually sees Kiyla sitting at a table with her hands on her head. She doesn't look too good. Jayla is a few feet away, dumping her lunch in the trash and then placing the tray above the garbage bin. As she makes her way back to the table where Kiyla is sitting, the group of girls from before gets in front of her. Jayla sighs, looking irritable. She doesn't make eye contact with the girls, who are blocking Jayla from interfering—the girl who Kiyla was arguing with earlier is standing behind Kiyla, who's sitting at the table and looking ill.

JAYLA PRICE. Would you just leave her alone! She wasn't herself.

GIRL, *talking to her posse.* Keep her away. (*Looks down at Kiyla.*) So. Not so tough now, huh?

KIYLA GERALD, *in a low tone.* Leave me alone.

Girl, *laughing.* What you start, you'll finish. (*Raises her hand, about to smack Kiyla.*)

ZADARION, *bumping into the girl and spilling his leftover food all over her clothes.* Oops. Girl, my bad.

GIRL, *looking disgusted.* No you did not just ruin my— (*Pushes Zadarion on the floor.*)

PRINCIPAL HARVIEL, *entering the cafeteria just in time and speaking loudly.* That's it! All of you—in my office now!

Principal Harviel walks toward the group of girls and directs them to his office, walking behind them. Janitor Marvello gathers Jayla and Kiyla as well and takes them to Harviel's office. After the group of girls is dealt their punishment, Harviel calls Jayla and Kiyla to come into his office. They closed the door behind them.

PRINCIPAL HARVIEL. This is disappointing. The only time you were in my office, Jayla, you and Zadarion had a disagreement. Glad to see you're friends now.

JAYLA PRICE, *sighing and rolling her eyes*. Whatever.

PRINCIPAL HARVIEL. Excuse me young lady?

JAYLA PRICE, *jumping out of the chair and bursting out in frustration*. Why are we in here anyway? *They* were the ones who started with *us*. Do your job and *punish them*!

PRINCIPAL HARVIEL. Should I remind you of the incident earlier this morning with your new friend … *Points to a sickly-looking Kiyla*. I want to know what's going on with the two of you. You and Kiyla never talk to that particular group of girls. What's going on lately?

JAYLA PRICE. Nothing okay. Can we just take whatever punishment you got for us so we can go?

PRINCIPAL HARVIEL, *loosening his tie and sighing*. They're not paying me enough for this. (*Looks at the two girls.*)

JAYLA PRICE, *shaking her head, annoyed and yells again*. Can we please just go! You obviously don't want anything.

PRINCIPAL HARVIEL. *Young lady*, would you watch your tone. I *will* go there with you. Now I repeat, what is going on with the two of you?

JAYLA PRICE, *sits back down next to Kiyla and sighs loudly*.

KIYLA GERALD, *still leaning to one side and holding her forehead*. I can't breathe. *Falls out of the chair and onto the floor*.

JAYLA PRICE, *jumping to her feet*. Kiyla!

PRINCIPAL HARVIEL, *getting out of his chair and rushing to Kiyla's side.* Call the nurse in here *now*!

Jayla runs to the secretary's office. The secretary immediately dials 9-1-1 from the office phone, and the paramedics arrived at Centransdale High School, in less than ten minutes, taking Kiyla Gerald to the local hospital in Hidendale Springs, IL, where doctors get to work on her immediately. Jayla's mother drives her to the hospital after school, and Jayla stays overnight, falling asleep in the waiting room. Jayla too was feeling ill, just not as bad as Kiyla.

Tuesday, May 30, 2107

The next morning, doctors told Jayla about an illegal substance in Kiyla's blood. They didn't know what it could be because there were many unusual compounds in the blood sample. There was no pinpointing exactly what could be causing Kiyla's illness. Kiyla woke up in the hospital bed, with no memory of the day before. Jayla could not remember anything either after she woke up in the waiting area.

JAYLA PRICE, *entering the hospital room Kiyla is in.* Knock, knock. *Peeks inside.* You doing okay?

KIYLA GERALD, *laughing.* Yeah. Just wish I can remember how I got here. *Sighs.* Do you know?

JAYLA PRICE, *closing the door and sitting at the end of the hospital bed.* Your doctor had a talk with me earlier. But I swear, after I woke up in the waiting area, I didn't even know how I got here. I heard your name so I figured you were in an accident. I feel like a horrible friend for not remembering.

KIYLA GERALD. You're a great friend if you ask me. Whatever it was, at least you're here with me right now. (*Smiles.*) Don't beat

154

yourself up, Jayla. (*Play slaps Jayla's arm.*) Zadarion needs to bring his butt here.

JAYLA PRICE. Yeah. (*Laughs.*)

Later on, Centransdale High School has just let out for the day. Zadarion is the last student to leave the school building, or so it feels that way. Zadarion went to the boy's restroom right before the bell rung. He leaves the restroom and heads to his locker to grab his things, planning to visit Jayla and Kiyla at the hospital. All of a sudden, he remembers he left something in Mr. Colusson's chemistry lab. He's not sure why he feels compelled to do so, but he goes to the restroom again but uses his V-Link to cloak himself before going to the lab. Zadarion peeks in the chemistry lab door's window and sees the spiky-haired boy, who also has black and reddish hair, Alecxander, inside the classroom. Zadarion watches him through the window.

ALECXANDER JACKSON, *sitting at a lab station/desk inside the chemistry lab*. A few more tests, and I'll be done for today. *Reaches to the floor for something in his book bag, and his elbow hits a test tube, knocking the contents on the floor.* Crap! *Gets out of his chair and goes into the walk-in closet, looking for cleaning supplies.*

A young girl is walking toward Mr. Colusson's chemistry lab. Zadarion backs up to the wall quietly, letting the girl pass. Having no idea Zadarion is standing by the door, the girl enters the lab, seeming to be in a panicky state of agitation.

MORGAN WILES, *entering the room and hurrying to her lab station/ desk*. I cannot believe I let it get out there. *Places things into her bag.*

Alecxander hears a voice and peeks out of the closet to see that his lab partner has entered the room, looking troubled. He waits a while, watching unseen.

ALECXANDER JACKSON, *exits the cleaning supply closet.* Oh hey, Morgan. What's got you so fidgety?

MORGAN WILES, *doesn't hear him and continues placing items into her bag.*

ALECXANDER JACKSON, *moving closer and tapping her shoulder.* Morgan?

MORGAN WILES, *jumping.* What!? *Calms down quickly.* Oh hey, Alec. What are you doing here?

ALECXANDER JACKSON, *looking at her quizzically.* I'm always here after school. You worried about something?

MORGAN WILES, *calm.* Nope. I'm good. *Starts to zip up her book bag, and a vial falls to the floor but, luckily, it doesn't break.* Shoot!

ALECXANDER JACKSON, *reaches to the floor to pick up the vial.*

MORGAN WILES. Don't worry about it. I got it.

ALECXANDER JACKSON. No, it's fine. (*Examines the vial.*) A failed science project? (*Looks at Morgan.*)

MORGAN WILES. Please hand it over, Alec.

ALECXANDER JACKSON. Why do you look like you're about to go to jail or something—? (*Starts to think.*) Wait a minute.

Alec has a mini flashback. There was a party at Morgan's house a few days ago. Kiyla and Jayla were invited to Morgan's nerd party. Alec snaps back to reality.

MORGAN WILES, *raising her voice.* Can I have my vial back please!?

ALECXANDER JACKSON. This is the project you've been working on for the past weeks. An elixir to make you popular? *Isn't entirely sure of what he's saying but is guessing based on how Morgan feels sometimes.*

MORGAN WILES. I don't know what you're talking about. Just give it back! *Reaches for her vial.*

ALECXANDER JACKSON, *pulling his arm back and stopping her from snatching the vial.* Hold on. *Has a puzzled expression on his face.* You didn't drug Kiyla and Jayla with this, did you?

MORGAN WILES. Why would I do that?

ALECXANDER JACKSON. Don't play dumb. You've had an obsession with Jayla for some time. Then your focus shifted to Kiyla when she started coming to our school.

MORGAN WILES. Again. I don't know what you're talking about. (*Attempts to snatch the vial again.*) Just give it *back*!

ALECXANDER JACKSON. No. I think Principal Harviel needs to know what you did.

MORGAN WILES. You would actually go there? You would snitch on your best friend ... your only friend? We always look out for each other.

ALECXANDER JACKSON, *hesitating for some time and thinking about letting his suspicions slide.* I— I— (*Looks at the floor.*)

MORGAN WILES, *grabs a syringe (resembling a vial too) out of her back pocket, inconspicuously, and holds it behind her back.*

ALECXANDER JACKSON. No. (*Shakes his head rapidly.*) I can't let you get away with that. (*Looks at her.*) You almost killed them. Yes, Jayla and Kiyla. That vial affected them in different ways.

MORGAN WILES. I know and I'm sorry for what I did. (*Sighs.*) I'm also sorry for this. (*Jumps and kicks Alec in his chest.*)

Alecxander falls on his back, but he quickly gets back to his feet. Morgan and Alec watch one another closely. Morgan keeps her focus on the vial in Alec's hand. Alec keeps his hand tightly around the vial. Morgan throws a couple punches at Alec. Alec leans back, left to right, dodging all her punches. Morgan stabs Alec with the syringe in her hand and pushes him down.

MORGAN WILES, *grabbing the vial out Alec's hand.* Enjoy a double dosage of the same formula Kiyla and Jayla had. I'm sorry, buddy, but I really got to go. *Grabs her book bag and exits the chemistry lab quickly.*

The lab door smacks a beyond-confused Zadarion in the face. Zadarion enters the lab, holding his throbbing face. He is now uncloaked. Alec is writhing frantically on the ground, yelling in pain. Sparks soon fly out of his body.

ZADARION, *his eyes widening.* It's *you! It has dawned on him that Alecxander is Shocker.*

Just before Zadarion has a chance to get closer to Alecxander, electricity starts to spark between the two boys. Two figures emerge from the sparks—the tall one gets up in Zadarion's face, shouting.

TUNDARICK. *He's acting out of control, enraged.* What you do to my brother? Answer me!

ZADARION, *is scared out of his wits and finds himself unable to make a sound.*

GAI, *standing beside Alecxander.* Enough, Tundarick. Leave the kid alone.

ZADARION, *thinking to himself.* Kid? You look like my age.

TUNDARICK, *pointing at Zadarion.* You be quiet.

GAI. Come. Pick Alec up. It seems whatever's affecting him is preventing his self-control. (*Sighs.*) We have to get him home, quickly.

TUNDARICK, *looks at Zadarion and growls before walking toward Alecxander and picking him up.*

GAI, *holding his arm up, eyes glowing, and saying an unfamiliar term.* Shoc'Tweil.

As the three of them disappear, the electricity in the room diminishes. Zadarion stands there, totally confused.

Gai and Tundarick take Alecxander back to their residence, to find a way to heal him.

Morgan Wiles runs down Tarainound Street in Hidendale Springs, making her way to the closest bus stop. Morgan plans to take the bus to the closest SpeedWay Rail Lines station, in Flavrare County, IL.

MORGAN WILES, *running and thinking aloud at the same time.* I gotta get out of here.

Morgan hears a voice coming from somewhere nearby, instructing her to cut through the alley. Morgan thinks it's her conscience and runs into the alley. A portal opens in front of her, and she immediately stops in front of it. Morgan stares at the portal and then something pushes her inside. The portal closes as a shadowy figure's chuckling slowly stops.

Morgan is in a dark place. She falls to the bottom of whatever it is.

MORGAN WILES, *standing up and looking around.* Where am I?

DiLusion, *hiding in the shadows so Morgan hears only a disembodied voice.* You're in DiLu-Land. *Emerges from the darkness.*

Morgan Wiles, *taking a few steps back.* Wha-what's wrong with your face? (*Is scared.*)

DiLusion. Don't be afraid. You may not be familiar with my ... sudden appearance, but I'm a friendly. I go by the name DiLusion.

Morgan Wiles, *defensively.* Why'd you bring me here?

DiLusion. You seem to be in some trouble.

Morgan Wiles, *playing dumb.* I don't know what you're talking about.

DiLusion, *circling Morgan.* You're lying. (*Smiles.*) Heheh. The virus that infected two of your fellow classmates—you had something to do with that, didn't you? (*Smiles like he already knows the answer.*)

Morgan Wiles. You know stalking is a federal crime?

DiLusion. And so is creating and distributing illegal dru–

Morgan Wiles, *she cuts him off and starts rolling her eyes.* You're creepy. Can you please let me out of whatever place this is?

DiLusion. Oh suuure. If you're positive about spending the rest of your teenage years in a federal prison. I highly doubt that you would want to go back there and spend the rest of your life running. Let me come out with why I brought you here. I need something from you.

Morgan Wiles, *giving him a confused look and then figuring out what he might want.* What do you want?

DiLusion. It's pretty easy. You're a smart girl. (*Stares before saying more.*) I need you to make more of that drug for me.

MORGAN WILES. *She raises her voice.* You're mad! It almost killed two of my classmates. What do you want something like that for?

DILUSION. Oh you are totally missing the point. (*Smirks, playing a game with Morgan, and then looks up into the vast emptiness above his head.*) You know, there won't be a place for you to hide, right? (*Looks serious and faces Morgan.*) Everywhere you go, someone will be watching.

MORGAN WILES, *starting to feel scared and alone.* I know. *Closes her eyes as tears fill them.*

DILUSION. I'm offering you assistance. You do a little work for me, and I'll help you clear this whole mess right on up.

MORGAN WILES, *sniffing, taking off her glasses, and wiping her eyes.* How can you help me? *Puts her glasses back on.*

DILUSION. Unlimited exposure to the truth. We're both scientists. What we invent may cause casualties, but in the end our intentions are good. I'll help you overcome this and return to your life.

MORGAN WILES, *thinking about her past.* I'd rather avoid that life.

DILUSION, *looking at her in a concerned, caring way.* Why?

MORGAN WILES. I don't want to think about my past okay?! (*Starts breathing rapidly.*) You help me get out of this mess, and I will give you this "Flurry" drug I created? That is what you want?

DILUSION. Not entirely. So, do we have a deal?

MORGAN WILES. Yes. (*Looks around.*) So, do you have any equipment to get me started making more?

DILUSION. I'll get you what you need. (*Smiles.*) Thank you.

MORGAN WILES. You're welcome.

There's something mysterious about this alien named DiLuAH who took over Lilori's mind. What are his intentions? What plans does DiLusion have in store for Morgan and the dangerous drug, the Flurry?

Thursday, June 1, 2107

Gai and Tundarick make it to their home in Kale County, just fifteen minutes south of Hidendale Springs. They live in a home on Nathom Street, down from the Iron Row Apartment Complex. Tundarick takes Alecxander up to his room and lays Alec on his bed. Gai is working on a way to alleviate Alec's pain.

TUNDARICK, *walking downstairs to the living room to speak with Gai, clearly angry.* That kid. I should've finished him off.

GAI, *sitting in the middle of the living room floor, his legs crossed, his hands in his lap, and his eyes closed.* Calm down. This was not the boy's fault. (*Sighs.*) I've never seen anything like this. (*Tries to connect to his ancestors' spirits for answers but cannot.*) Arrrgggghhhh. (*Stands up.*) This is impossible! After my reincarnation, my tether to the spirit world has been severed. I don't know how I can find a cure for poor Alec. (*Looks at the ceiling, toward Alec's room.*)

TUNDARICK, *paces back and forth, shaking his head from side to side.*

GAI, *stops suddenly.* I got it.

TUNDARICK. What's the plan?

GAI. Herbal medicine with a little something extra.

TUNDARICK, *looks confused.*

Gai heads upstairs to Alec's room. Tundarick follows. In Alec's room, Gai sees that Alec is still in pain. He is holding his chest, where his heart is located, and writhing around in his bed. Gai approaches Alec's body. Tundarick waits by the door. Gai places his hands out in front of him. From the looks of it, Alec doesn't even know Gai is there. He is suffering too much.

GAI. Hold on, young Alec. *Moves his hands over Alec's writhing body, closes his eyes, and concentrates.*

Gai is channeling his inner electricity. His fingers start to spark. A tiny lightning storm starts above Alec's chest. Alec's body begins to calm down. Soon, he is lying motionless. Gai stops channeling and lowers his hands to his sides.

TUNDARICK, *approaching a motionless Alec.* Shall I grab the herbal medicine?

GAI, *continuing to watching Alec.* I lied about that. He should be fine now. Let him rest it off.

TUNDARICK, *concerned.* What did you do to him?

GAI, *starts to walk toward the door.* The lightning I channeled fried the poison inside Alec's body—at least I hope so. *Walks out of Alec's room, looking disappointed.*

TUNDARICK, *speaking very softly.* What? *Follows Gai out of Alec's room and goes downstairs.*

Gai and Tundarick sit in front of the television and wait for Alec to get better.

Season 1, Episode 7

Mission Stop 5,000-Pound Bomb

Friday, June 2, 2107

It is 4:00 in the evening, and Max Gerald is locked away in Gowdon's Prison, in Flavrare County, IL. A man in an all-black suit, wearing a black hat, enters the facility. After being processed by the prison guards, the man is escorted to Max's cell. All the other inmates are either resting in their beds or hanging around in the recreation room. The man approaches Max's cell.

STURGESS MCMILLAN, *in a stern, deep voice.* Good evening, Mr. Gerald.

MAX GERALD, *lying in his bed and looking at the top bunk.* Ugh. Man, I don't know that guy. There's only Myers in here, aka Max. *Pauses.* What do you want, suit?

STURGESS MCMILLAN. My name is Sturgess McMillan. I work with the organization known as ZEXTERN.

MAX GERALD, *standing up, looking out of his cell, and staring at Sturgess.* Never heard of it. I repeat, suit. What do you want?

MR. MCMILLAN. I would like to hire you for a job.

MAX GERALD. Yeah, why not? Sure, suit. One problem with that. *Grabs the cell bars, raising his voice.* You gonna get me outta here?!

MR. MCMILLAN. Your release papers are being processed right now. Meet me at the front gate when the paperwork has gone through. *Turns and walks away from Max's cell. The prison guard, who's standing by the exit door, lets him out.*

Max Gerald, *licking his lips and smiling.* Early bail. Heh, heh.

Mr. McMillan is waiting outside of the facility, leaning on the passenger side of his vehicle, a 2109 Maserati GliJis PWS, which is basically a 2014 Maserati Ghibli RWD, except it has a stretch body with double doors for passengers on each side of the rear. A driver is sitting in the driver's seat. Max Gerald steps outside of the facility through the side exit, his paperwork successfully completed. A guard posted at the exit shuts the door behind Max.

Exit Guard Watch. You'll be back, you psycho. Up in that same cell too.

Max Gerald keeps walking toward Mr. McMillan's vehicle. He is thinking about burning the guard alive with the metallic lighter that is hanging on the guard's belt. In his mind, Max laughs hysterically as the guard burns. He reaches the vehicle within nine seconds, stops to admire the car, and then looks at Mr. McMillan and smiles.

Mr. McMillan, *a serious look on his face.* Are you ready?

Max Gerald. So what's this job you got for me?

Mr. McMillan, *turning around, walking to the rear of the car, and opening one of the side doors.* I'll tell you at the office. Get in the vehicle. (*Slides into the vehicle.*)

Max Gerald stops smiling and gets into the vehicle, which drives off, heading away from the facility.

Six hours later, Zadarion is alone at the arcade in Hidendale Springs playing video games. After playing for an hour (four o'clock in the evening) Zadarion decides to leave. Without Sam, the arcade isn't the same anymore. Zadarion walks down Tarainound Street, heading home. He's four blocks from his home when his V-Link activates. Just then, a K1500 4x4 truck speeds down Tarainound Street, passing Zadarion, who is on the sidewalk. Zadarion watches as the truck smashes into NH Pharmacy. A man jumps out of the truck and runs into the nearest alleyway, and seconds later, the truck explodes. Zadarion flinches and looks on in horror. He hears screams but not many, as many people are not in the area. Zadarion remains froze in place, completely motionless. His V-Link activates again and vibrates three times. Zadarion finally snaps out of his dazed state, grabs hold of his V-Link, and runs into the alleyway. Just as he makes it to the alleyway, two ambulances arrive at the scene, screeching to a stop in front of the burning pharmacy. Shortly thereafter, three fire trucks arrive and park behind the ambulances. Firefighters rush out of the trucks to put out the fire, and paramedics jump from the ambulances, gurneys in hand, and stop twenty feet in front of the building. Zadarion ducks farther into the alleyway, being sure to remain hidden. He is too late to catch the fleeing terrorist. His V-Link activates and vibrates. He grabs it and holds it out in front of him. A hologram version of Commander Addams pops out.

COMMANDER ADDAMS, *appearing as a hologram.* Report to VLORs immediately, Z. *The hologram disappears.*

A firefighter, positioned on the outskirts of the scene to keep people away from the fire, spots Zadarion in the alleyway and reaches for his walkie. Zadarion uses his V-Link and materializes a Dabney Dart, which is used to make individuals faint. Zadarion swiftly throws the dart at the fireman, hitting him in the neck, and the man topples to the ground. Zadarion teleports to VLORs.

After the bombing of the local pharmacy on Tarainound Street, Z, Rahz, and Caj have all been summoned to VLORs to attend a briefing with Commander Addams.

Z arrives at VLORs and makes his way to the operations room. He's approaching the entrance when he hears footsteps behind him. He turns and sees Rahz.

AGENT Z, *looking at Rahz.* Hey.

AGENT RAHZ. Hey.

Caj is making his way to the operations room as well. Z and Rahz hear Caj's footsteps and look down the hallway. Just as Caj stops at the entrance, the intercom system turns on. A red flashing dot blinks steadily.

COMMANDER ADDAMS, *addressing the entire ship over the intercom system.* Attention on board Attention on board. Agents Z, Rahz, and Caj, make your way to the operations room at this time.

The intercom system beeps four times and clicks off. The operations room doors slide open, and the three agents enter. Commander Addams enters the room five minutes later. The doors close behind him. One of the operators, sitting at their workstation, presses a button on their keyboard, and a thin television screen lowers in the center of the room from the ceiling. The television screen turns itself on, and video footage of the recent bombing in Hidendale Springs appears on the screen. Rahz looks away. Z looks at the floor. Caj never bothers to look at the screen.

AGENT CAJ, *looking at Z and then turning his head to look at Commander Addams.* Who did this?

COMMANDER ADDAMS. I have some private operatives looking deeply into this terrorist attack. (*Looks at Z.*) Agent Z, this is a part of your sector. Do you feel comfortable with this assignment?

AGENT Z, *gulping.* People died. (*Is scared.*) I was right there, and I couldn't move my body to act.

AGENT CAJ. Fear took hold over you Z.

COMMANDER ADDAMS. This is why I ask. You may decline this assignment if you feel uncomfortable. I'll just put ano—

AGENT Z, *interrupting the commander.* No! That's not it. (*Inhales and exhales slowly.*) I'll find this terrorist. I promise.

COMMANDER ADDAMS. Do not promise. You got this. Good luck. (*Looks at the three agents and turns his attention to Rahz.*) Rahz, you be especially watchful in your sector. We do not know if this was an actual attack on the US government or against VLORs. So, all of you. (*Addresses everyone in the operations room.*) Be more discreet, cautious. and observant in your everyday activities.

The three agents nod their heads at Commander Addams, who nods and then walks out of the operations room.

Saturday, June 3, 2107

Max Gerald is inside a subway station in Dowers City, IL. The subway station is deserted at this time of day. The company, the ones who hired Max Gerald, paid the city to have the subway station shut down for a while.

Four masked men holding Mk47s are assisting Max. Suddenly, the lights in the subway station flicker on and off. Max grins and looks around. The four masked men raise their Mk47s and swing them around, trying to locate the culprit. Z jumps down from the subway station's ceiling and knocks out the four armed individuals. Then he flips over Max's head. Max ducks low, trying to avoid being hit in the face. Z lands on the other side of Max and stands, staring at Max, who stares back and grins.

MAX GERALD. Way to go! *Claps his hands together a couple times and laughs maniacally.*

AGENT Z. You're the one. (*Materializes his blaster from his V-Link and into his right hand.*) Whatever you're doing here, you won't get away with it.

MAX GERALD. Oh! You mean the bomb I attached to this train? (*Points to the train at his right and then lowers his hand back to his side.*) Heh, heh.

AGENT Z, *clenching his left fist and squeezing his blaster tightly in his right hand.* You killed innocent people. (*Shouts.*) Why?

MAX GERALD. You know. It's funny. (*Pulls out a gun from under his shirt.*)

The four masked men slowly start to wake up and pick themselves off the ground.

MAX GERALD. If you're going to neutralize someone, why not do it right.

Max pulls out a gun and shoots the four masked men, killing them. Max raises the gun to his mouth and blows the smoke away. Z looks scared and a little confused. He raises his blaster, pointing it at Max, and Max lowers the gun.

MAX GERALD. Aw. Why so blue? I did you a favor. No more witnesses. (*Laughs maniacally.*)

AGENT Z, *keeping his blaster pointed at Max.* You maniac.

MAX GERALD. Come on. Shoot me. Kill me. Kill me, Mr. Secret Agent boy. (*Laughs.*)

AGENT Z, *remaining motionless and keeping an eye on Max.* Our blasters are not for killing people.

Max Gerald. Oh what's the fun in that? (*Yawns.*) Well, if you don't mind, I reeeeally gotta get this train moving.

Agent Z, *shouting.* No!

Agent Z runs straight toward Max. He jumps and kicks Max in his chest, sending him sprawling to the ground on his face. Max rolls on his back. Z hovers over Max and points his blaster directly at Max's head. Max is on the ground, laughing hysterically, daring Z to do it.

Max Gerald. Yay. He's gonna do it! (*Laughs.*)

Agent Z, *shouting.* Shut up, butthead! (*Keeps his blaster pointed at Max's head.*)

The train's engine turns on, and the train starts moving on its own, quickly gaining speed. Max laughs hysterically. Z turns his head, looking at the train speeding away and then looks back at Max.

Max Gerald. Heh, heh. What're you gonna do? Stand over me or stop a moving bomb from reaching its destination …College Station, TX. (*Laughs hysterically.*)

Z contemplates which is more important. Should he capture Max now or go after the train? Ten seconds pass, and Z makes his decision. He slaps Max across his face with his blaster, knocking him out and then materializes his flight board and jumps on it. He floats in midair and then flies after the speeding train, trying to think of a way to bring the train to a halt without setting the bomb.

Sometime after Agent Z chased after the train, Max gets to his feet, having faked the unconsciousness. He massages his head, pulls out a cell phone, and calls his boss to come pick him up.

Max Gerald, *talking on the phone.* This job is done. I need a ride from the subway station in Dowers City. (*Ends the call and puts the cellular phone in his pocket. He walks up the stairs and exits the subway station.*)

Z is still following the speeding train on his flight board when he receives a call from VLORs. He answers the call.

Commander Addams, *on his headset.* What are you doing, Z? A train is speeding toward College Station, TX.

Agent Z. I know. I'm in pursuit. I don't know how to stop it without the train exploding.

Commander Addams. I have your signal here following a different train. I'll send you these coordinates so you'll see for yourself. It includes both trains and the distances they are apart from each other.

Agent Z. What!? I've been following a decoy? (*Stops his fight board in midair.*)

Commander Addams. Stop that train and hurry to catch the other one. (*Ends the call.*)

Agent Z. This was a diversion. Agh. (*Remains high up in the sky, looking down at the moving train he has been following, still trying to figure out how he's going to stop the train with the bomb.*) Agh. This is so frustrating.

Rahz, hovering four inches off the ground, is skating toward the speeding train.

Agent Rahz. Go on ahead, Z. I got this.

Agent Z. Appreciate it!

Rahz uses her boots to jump high into the air. When she is close to Z's flight board, she flips, twirls her body, and then does a backflip, aiming for the train. Z flies past the train he was following, trying to catch up to the other one. Z checks his V-Link for the train's exact coordinates. He locates the other train and sees that it's approximately three states away. Z's V-Link activates, and his flight board locks his feet into position. The flight board picks up speed faster, edging closer to the other train. Z wishes there was some way he could teleport with his flight board.

Meanwhile, Rahz materializes her daggers and points them out in front of her. She shoots lightning out of her daggers at the ground to keep herself airborne and rides the wind, landing on top of the train. She lies on the top of the train, her arms and legs stretched out, points her daggers to each side, and sends electricity out. The excess electricity reaches the trains wheels, and the train starts to skid on the tracks.

Z is now a few cities away from the speeding train. His V-Link allows his flight board to pick up a little more speed. After twenty minutes, Z finally reaches the train. He passes it, turns around on his fight board, and flies straight at it. He breaks through the conductor's window, and his flight board dematerializes into his V-Link.

Agent Z. I have to find this bomb, quick.

Having stopped the other train and hurried to catch up to Z, Rahz enters the train Z is on by blasting a hole in the side of a cargo hold area. She walks into the next unit and sees Z.

Agent Rahz. Did you check the status of the engine room yet?

Agent Z, *looking embarrassed.* Oh no. I didn't.

Z pulls out his V-Link and runs a quick scan to check for problems in the train's engine or for anything unusual that might be aboard. When the scan is complete, no bomb has been detected on board. The cargo holds room is empty as well.

AGENT Z, *panicking.* Where's this bomb!?

AGENTS RAHZ. It's here somewhere.

AGENT Z. It's not inside the train. Where is— *(Stops short, his mouth dropping open.)* The train. It's a bomb.

AGENT RAHZ, *her eyes widening in shock, and then viewing the train's specs in her V-Link.* It appears the bomb was embedded into the train. We have to abandon ship.

AGENT Z. Yeah, I agree. It's a good thing there are no passengers on board.

Rahz and Z jump out of the moving train. Z materializes his fight board and jumps on it. Rahz's V-Link activates the hovering ability in her boots. Z flies directly alongside the moving train, trying to reach the front. Rahz skates four inches off the ground, following Agent Z.

AGENT RAHZ. Z, catch. (*Throws a valve container to Z.*)

AGENT Z, *stopping his flight board and turning around to catch the valve container with his right hand.* What is this? (*Examines it.*)

AGENT RAHZ. Don't worry about what it is. Take it to the front of the train and toss it on the tracks.

Z has no other option but to listen to Rahz. Z flies ahead of the train, turns his flight board around, and tosses the valve container onto the tracks. A special chemical bursts out of the valve, causing the tracks to part and extend upward. Rahz skates toward the train, holding one of her daggers in her right hand. She stops in front of the moving train and quickly extends her left arm out in front of her. A charge of electricity shoots out of her dagger, striking the train's front wheels. The train skids, creating a lot of sparks and slows down, finally comes to a halt sixty seconds later. Z tosses an Invisi-Dome that covers the entire train. The train explodes. After four minutes, the smoke clears, and the Invisi-Dome disappears.

AGENT Z, *landing right next to Rahz and dematerializing his flight board.* Thanks for your help. (*Breathes heavy.*)

AGENT RAHZ. No problem, scaredy boy.

AGENT Z. What? (*Thinks about something smart to say back. He comes up with nada.*)

AGENT RAHZ. Relax. I'm only kidding. (*Nods her head at Z.*) See you back at the ship. (*Teleports away from the area.*)

AGENT Z, *cracking his knuckles.* Oh, I'm going to put you away, Max Gerald. *Teleports away from the area.*

Tuesday, June 6, 2107

Mr. Sturgess McMillan's vehicle arrives at Skyyas Airport in Laroouse City, IL, about an hour and thirty minutes west of Valousse City, IL. The vehicle's driver parks across the street near the edge. Mr. McMillan orders his driver to roll up the glass window that separates the vehicle's driver and passenger seats. Mr. McMillan explains Max's new assignment, and once he's agreed to all the terms and responsibilities, Mr. McMillan's driver stops and lets him out of the vehicle. Agent Z is cloaked, thanks to his V-Link, and hiding in plain sight behind a flagpole. He's holding his V-Link out in front of him, and a red light is flashing on the V-Link's automatic pop-up screen. Z tagged Max at the subway station a few days ago.

Agent Z. I got you now. You slick little punk. (*Follows Max, keeping a close eye on him.*)

Max enters the airport through the entrance's rotating doors. A cloaked Agent Z continues to follow him inside. Z locates a spot on the ceiling from which he'll be able to keep a close watch on Max. He activates his eye scanner, located on his headset, in order to zoom in closer on Max's location through solid walls. Max loafs around for two hours, sitting in the airport's waiting area. Z is determined to stop him before he commits another heinous crime.

AGENT Z, *looking through his eye scanner and whispering to himself.* Any time now.

After Z has waited at the airport for almost three hours, he sees a man in a clean suit walk up to Max and sit down in the chair across from him. The man reaches across the table and shakes Max's hand. Agent Z recognizes the man.

AGENT Z, *watching the two men talking, his body still cloaked.* Monroe. (*Is confused.*) What is the Indian casino guy doing here?

CLOUDIS MONROE. I see the organization continues to hire gentlemen of your …caliber. (*Speaking in an offensive manner.*)

MAX GERALD. Heh heh. (*Reaches inside of his left pocket, pulls out a round spear-like object, and places it on the table.*) Trade for trade? Heh, heh.

AGENT Z, *zooming in close to study the spear-like object.* What is that?

An elderly man walks past Max and Monroe's table, holding a briefcase. Max turns his head for a second to look at the guy and then looks back at Monroe, smiling.

CLOUDIS MONROE. I am glad not to be that organization's lapdog anymore. Poor guy. (*Reaches in his left chest pocket, pulling out a thin, black box, and hands it to Max. Takes the spear-like object off the table and pockets it.*) We're done here. (*Stands up, pushing the chair under the table.*) Oh. A piece of advice. Try to avoid making a scene this time.

Cloudis Monroe walks away. Max shakes his head, grinning. Max stands up, placing the thin, black box in his right pants pocket. He looks around, trying to locate the elderly man who passed by him earlier. Max walks closer to the elderly man, moving very slowly. The elderly man is enjoying his croissant and freshly made coffee. Max stops walking and stands in the center of the airport. He removes the gun from his back pants pocket, extends his right arm up, and shoots the ceiling. Everyone in the airport stares at him and then panics.

MAX GERALD. Attention all you wealthy snobs. There's a man in this here airport who must pay for his disloyalty. I'm feeling extremely bad today. So guess what? You all will pay for his mistakes. (*Laughs.*)

A shot is fired at the floor where Max is standing. Everyone is panicking, covering themselves and their children. Max looks at his shoes. A thin, metallic line wraps around his right wrist and pulls him out of the airport. Max drops the gun on the floor. He is being pulled through the air by an invisible force.

A mile away from the airport, near a cornfield, the thin, metallic line releases Max's right wrist, and Max falls out of the sky. Something swoops by and grabs him. It flies lower and drops Max on the ground. He gets to his feet, dusting himself off and laughing hysterically.

Max Gerald, *stopping to dust himself off and, staring left to right, beginning to laugh.* I know it's youuuu. (*Has a big smile on his face.*)

The invisibility wears off, and Z is standing twenty feet away from Max, staring him down.

Max Gerald. Oh Boy! (*Claps his hands in excitement and then stops.*) Well, what are you waiting for? I'm unarmed. Heh heh.

Agent Z, *starting to walk closer to Max and then stopping seven feet away from him.* I wasn't going to let you harm the old man at the airport.

Max Gerald. Pfft. You pansy. But I have no idea what you're talking about. (*Laughs and winks.*)

Z clenches his fists, launches forward, and punches Max in his jaw. Max hits the ground hard. He gets to his hands and knees, laughing hysterically. Z stands over Max, clenching his fists.

Max Gerald, *looking at the dirt on the ground.* You'll never stop their plans. (*Grabs a handful of dirt and throws it into Z's face and then stands up, still laughing.*)

Agent Z. Ahhh. *Backs away from Max, rubbing his eyes.*

Max Gerald. The itsy bitsy insect went up the water*spout.* (*Punches Z across his face.*) Down came the rain and washed the spider *out!* (*Punches Z in his spine.*)

Max Gerald starts punching with more speed and accuracy, clocking Z in his face and in his chest multiple times. Z leans his upper body slightly toward the ground, and Max knees him in his face. Z falls on the ground, covering his face and lower midsection, as he takes multiple blows, enduring Max's attacks. Max accidentally kicks Z's V-Link, and it activates its defensive mechanism. The V-Link sends Max flying backward. Z quickly stands up, shakes himself off, and speeds at Max. Z reaches Max, who's still in the air flying backward, and swings his right fist into Max's stomach. The blow sends Max straight to the ground, and he lands on his back hard. Z lands on the ground as well, holding a pair of V-Cuffs in his left hand. Max slowly rolls onto his stomach, coughing and trying to laugh. Z raises his left arm out in front of him, over Max's body, and he drops the V-Cuffs. The V-Cuffs fall on Max's back, wrap around his body, and immobilize him. Z taps his headset and calls VLORs.

COMMANDER ADDAMS, *on his headset*. Report.

AGENT Z. The terrorist is going to Gowdon's Prison.

COMMANDER ADDAMS. That's a negative. Bring him here, now. Caj will lead you to the interrogation center upon your arrival. Meet him in the Geared'NReady room.

AGENT Z. Aye, aye.

COMMANDER ADDAMS. See you at VLORs. (*Ends the call.*)

Z teleports himself and an immobilized Max to VLORs, arriving in the Geared'NReady room, and Caj helps him take an immobilized Max to the interrogation center, a dark room. When a criminal, or anyone else is brought here, he or she is unable to see the interrogator. Once inside the interrogation center, Max Gerald's body is propped upright against a wall, and the V-Cuffs are magnetized to the wall. Commander Addams enter the interrogation center, and the doors close and locks behind him.

COMMANDER ADDAMS. Caj, you may begin to get answers from this guy.

AGENT CAJ. Aye, aye, sir. (*Walks up to the immobilized Max Gerald and uses his V-Link to bring him back.*)

MAX GERALD, *moving his head, left to right, and laughing*. You guys like dark places. It's fine. I don't care about your identities anyway.

AGENT CAJ. Shut up. You will answer my questions truthfully. If you don't, I will make your life even worse than it already is.

MAX GERALD, *excitedly*. Oh sure. Whatever do you wish to know? I'll tell you everything. Heh heh.

Agent Z looks at Max like he wants to punch him. Commander Addams thinks Max is a lunatic. Caj has his usual "whatever" look on his face.

AGENT CAJ. Okay, first question. Why bomb the pharmacy located on Tarainound Street?

MAX GERALD. The organization, ZEXTERN hired me to do the job. The owner, Daniel Sahl, was a former contact of the organization. He was a traitor. Stole lots of files. Ugh, I don't know what he wanted with those. (*Shakes his head and smiles, looking at Caj.*) But hey, he's dead now! Heh-heh.

AGENT CAJ, *looking at Commander Addams and then back at Max*. Okay, next question. What's with the bomb being put into the train's system in Dowers City?

MAX GERALD. Oh we going in order are we? (*Laughs.*) The owner of a fuel company has been going crazy these days. ZEXTERN wanted to eliminate the new owner. He was overpricing them, obviously. Oh, and as for why I was at the airport, I met with Cloudis Monroe. You know him I'm sure. Well, the guy who hired me, Sturgess McMillan, used to be his boss. Unfortunately, he did not want him killed. I don't know why. I mean I would definitely like to kill the man because Cloudis is a douche, seriously. Sturgess wanted the black box back. Cloudis stole it.

AGENT CAJ. That black box is worthless. We sent it up to our scientists.

MAX GERALD. Oh! It's worth more than you think. *He winks.*

AGENT Z, *blurting out his question*. What about the old man you were going to kill?

Max Gerald. Oh him. (*Laughs.*) Former US General Thomas Eisenberg. He's not very well known, but he started ZEXTERN. I think that's right? (*Pauses for a while to think and then starts laughing.*) Well, long story short, Eisenberg was a traitor. So, anymore questions? (*Smiles at them.*)

Agent Caj. You know this ZEXTERN will be coming after you now, right? If they're this secretive, I'm guessing they will know whether or not you snitched.

Max Gerald, *grinning*. We'll see. (*Starts to laugh maniacally.*)

Commander Addams. All right. We've heard enough. Get him out of here.

Agent Caj. Sir, to Primous Facility? I say he'll be one perfect fit.

Commander Addams. Yes, what I was thinking. Also, we will look further into this ZEXTERN organization and the three others he mentioned. I've never once heard of them. (*Looks at Z.*) You did good, Z. Return home and wait for future assignments.

Agent Z. Aye, aye, sir. (*Walks to the door.*)

Max Gerald. Aww, but I'll miss you so much, Z. (*Laughs.*)

Agent Caj. Okay, that's enough out of you. (*Uses his V-Link to fully immobilize Max again.*)

Somewhere located in Dowers City, IL, at VICE headquarters, Commander General Talgitx is making his way back to his office when, all of a sudden, the lights flicker for a second.

Talgitx, *stopping*. Mario Vega. You better get VICE working properly. (*Isn't happy.*)

A portion of the wall to Talgitx's left slides open, revealing a hidden room on board VICE. Talgitx walks into the open space, and the wall slides back in place, closing Talgitx inside. He walks down a long hallway, finally reaching some stairs that head down. Talgitx walks down a long flight of stairs, finally making it to the bottom after five minutes. The lights, activated by motion sensors, turn on once Talgitx steps off the last stairs. Talgitx looks up and sees a room. Searching farther into the room, he sees someone inside a machine, but the person is wearing a helmet that covers his or her face. Talgitx walks closer to get a better view of the machine. The technology resembles that of a modified hospital bed, but with a covering over it. It is upright, so the person is standing. What could this mean for VICE?

TALGITX, *examining the modified hospital bed.* Why were you placed here, stranger? *He knit his eyebrows.*

Talgitx looks around this hidden room for a few more hours before finding a way out. Luckily the wall where he entered opened back up. He walks to his office.

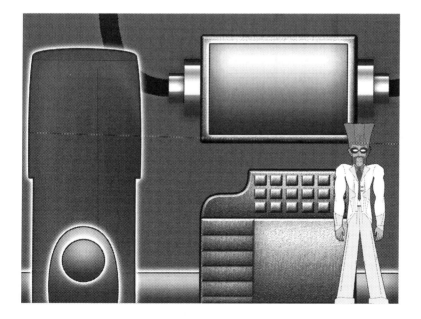

Meanwhile, in Kale County, IL, fifteen minutes south of Hidendale Springs. In the home on Nathom Street, down from the Iron Row Apartment Complex, Gai and Tundarick wait for Alec to wake. Alec lies motionless, in a deep sleep.

Alec finds himself surround by several others of his kind. There is a war going on. Jets are flying around the city dropping bombs. Alec sees people running away and others fighting back. Those who are fighting back are channeling electricity from their bodies and trying to shoot the jets. A jet flies over Alec's head. The people around him are screaming. They are scared. A bomb goes off nearby, and then Alec's vision goes dark and becomes cloudy. After a few seconds, Alec's vision clears, and he's surrounded by dead bodies. He begins to hyperventilate.

ALECXANDER, *hyperventilating as he stands among the dead bodies.* No. (*Shakes his head.*) Noooooooooooooooooooooo! (*Closes his eyes and screams out.*)

Several seconds later, silence falls. Alec opens his eyes. It's really dark. Even though he can't see in front of him, Alec stares straight into the distance. He feels something calling him, even if there is only silence. Alec starts to see bluish sparks coming from something far away—something that starts moving in closer, as if it is running. Alec starts breathing rapidly. The figure jumps high and lands in front of Alec. It puts its face in Alec's face and roars. Alec wakes up. His body jerks up, and he is hyperventilating. Tundarick is standing at Alec's bedroom door, watching him. Sitting in his bed, Alec looks horrified. Tundarick looks at him, wondering why he has had another nightmare. Alec raises his head and sees Tundarick standing by his bedroom door. Tundarick doesn't greet him.

ALECXANDER, *controlling his breathing.* Oh hey, brother. W-what's up?

TUNDARICK, *turning around to exit Alec's room.* Gai has to meditate with you more. *Shuts Alec's bedroom door behind him as he leaves his room.*

Alec lowers his head and closes his eyes for mere seconds. Alec sees eyes, with blue electricity coming from them. They are taunting him. His body jerks and he opens his eyes.

ALECXANDER. Who is that? Why am I having these weird thoughts? (*Grabs his head.*) Nooooo.

Season 1, Episode 8:
End of the year

Friday, June 9, 2107

Techy Andrew "Andy" Mathessen is sitting outside a coffee house in Paris, France. He has received schematics from a contact here and was sent to retrieve the schematics. He is taking a break to have a meal. He doesn't know he's being followed. After downloading new specs and programs into his tablet computer, Techy Andy finishes his coffee and responds to an e-mail he received earlier. After sending the e-mail, Techy Andy stands up and leaves a generous tip for the waitress on the table. He attaches his tablet computer to the hoister located on his right wrist and starts walking down the cobblestone sidewalk. After twenty minutes, he reaches the edge of town. His flight device activates, and he flies high up into the sky and away from the area.

An unknown, invisible agent watches him fly away. He swipes a section on his V-Link and activates the flight ability in his boots. Dust disperses in the area where the invisible agent was standing. The agent takes off into the sky, following Techy Andy.

Meanwhile, in Hidendale Springs, three school buses are parked outside of Hidendale Observatory. The students inside the buses, from Centransdale High School, are extremely excited about what awaits them inside. Curtis Anaheim walks out of the Observatory's front entrance, along with a male and a female tour guide. The male tour guide parts from the other two and heads toward a group of elderly civilians. The students exit the school buses and line up single file. Curtis Anaheim stands in front of the students with a smile on his face. The female tour guide, who's standing shoulder to shoulder with Anaheim, addresses the group of young teens. She has an intriguing smile on her face—one that raises suspicion—but she delivers it with the utmost politeness.

Ms. Cynthia Hadolsby. Good afternoon, Centransdale High freshman and sophomore students. My name is Cynthia Hadolsby. I'll be your tour guide today. How is everybody doing today?

Cynthia Hadolsby is a happy woman in her midthirties. She dresses professionally. She loves to wear plaid skirts that fall below her knees. Her blouses have to be of a solid color and neatly pressed. If a shirt is wrinkled, she throws a hissy fit. Despite her suspicious smile, she's pretty much a respectable woman.

Male Student, *shouting.* Great, ma'am!

Female Student, *also shouting.* Last day of school. Woohooo!

Ms. Cynthia Hadolsby, *acting like she didn't know.* So, this is your big end-of-the-year school trip. How fascinating. I will certainly make sure that this tour is ridiculously insane!

Mr. Curtis Anaheim, *joking.* But still fun I hope?

Ms. Cynthia Hadolsby. Why of course, Mr. Anaheim. (*Clears her throat.*) Where are my manners? (*Looks at the students.*) Now, students, this is Mr. Curtis Anaheim. He is the director and CEO of Anaheim Industries.

Zadarion is in the middle of the crowd of students. He is hoping to get a closer look at Anaheim's newest creation. Anaheim Industries unveils a new creation to the public every six months. Today marks the sixth-month release date. Unfortunately, nothing has been announced …yet. Zadarion keeps his fingers crossed.

Ms. Cynthia Hadolsby, *pleasantly.* Well, let's get the day started. Everyone into the Observatory. Hurry, hurry.

All the students head through the observatory's front entrance. Mr. Anaheim and Ms. Hadolsby wait until all the students are inside the building before following them in.

The male tour guide leads his group into the building fifteen minutes after Mr. Anaheim walked inside the building.

Two hours later, Techy Andy is flying over the Atlantic Ocean when he receives a phone call from someone important. The unknown agent, who's remaining invisible while flying, is a short distance behind him.

TECHY ANDY, *answering his phone.* I will be arriving back in the States within a few hours. The schematics are in my possession.

UNKNOWN CALLER. Very good. Make sure you stop by Hidendale Observatory to pick up a much needed tool. This should also help to bring my son back to his senses. I'll be awaiting your arrival, Mr. Mathessen.

TECHY ANDY. Yeah. I expect compensation for this assignment. (*Snickers.*)

UNKNOWN CALLER. You will be well compensated for your work. I keep my promises.

TECHY ANDY, *ends the call and continues onward toward the states.*

One hour later, a cloaked mystery agent is flying around Hidendale Springs, IL. The mystery agent's V-Link, which is following Techy Andy's scent, directs him to Hidendale Observatory. He lost Tech Andy at some point while flying over the Atlantic Ocean and New Waii Island before making it to the United States, and he's not sure how that happened. Deciding to follow his V-Link and search for Andy in the observatory, he lands on the observatory's roof. He swipes a section on his V-Link to change his appearance.

The mystery person makes his way downstairs and into the observatory without paying an entrance fee. He slips in among the group of students who are touring the observatory with Ms. Hadolsby, who has her back turned as she explains a meteorite on display in front of her.

to be continued ...

Appendix 1

Places
Cities, Towns, and States

Hidendale Springs, Illinois (thirty minutes north of Dowers City, IL)

- Hidendale Observatory (home of an *all new* exhibit with twenty planets on display
- Centransdale High School
- Tarainound Street (the main street, lined with many restaurants and convenience stores)
- Drekal Park District (the closest park to Tarainound Street, with many art pieces in the center of the park)
- Narthaniel Park District (the closest park to Himswelm Street, with one walkway and a children's park)
- Abigail's Home for Youths Foster Care (located on Himswelm Street next to Narthaniel Park District)
- Drenden Mountain (located behind Hidendale Observatory, with a cursed knight buried deep underneath it)
- Marquee Arcade (The only arcade in town, filled with a wide variety of video games, including virtual games, two-player games, and more)
- Maxie's Bar & Grill (located down the street from arcade)

Kale County, Illinois (fifteen minutes south of Hidendale Springs, IL)

- Kris Helmsdale Recreational hall
- Governor Stephan Gunneim's place of birth
- Iron Row Apartment Complex
- Stratum Oil Industries (third office location)
- Home of the elderly Mrs. Amelia Daggerton (currently ill), the mother of Pesto've Daggerton and Darius Helms
- Mitchel Street

Dowers City, Illinois (thirty minutes south of Hidendale Springs, IL)

- VICE secret warehouse (where VICE scientists constructed many electronic emitters and the place that destroyed DiLusion)
- Dale's Shopping Center (Home of a few name brand clothing stores and quality restaurants)
- Diamond and Ore Okiewa Chemical factory (located in the little forest of Dowers City)
- Q National Bank
- Quail Street

Flavrare County (Town), Illinois (fifteen minutes north of Valousse City, IL)

- Gravers Street (location of the secret home and secret laboratory of Scientist Kelo Ritz)
- Mackie's Donuts Store
- Gowdon's Prison (houses many inmates for all sorts of crimes)
- Lexus Street (near a wide, open field, just down from Mackie's Donuts Store)
- Iris's Fashion Jewelry Store
- SpeedWay Rail Lines (SpeedWay Rail Train going in and out of the town)

Valousse City, Illinois (thirty minutes south of Dowers City, IL)

- Lincoln Oaks Mall (a huge shopping center with great but mostly expensive stores and a very few affordable ones)
- Anaheim Industries: Applied Sciences Division (Curtis Anaheim, owner and CEO)
- Lorisdale National Park (has trails lined with art sculptures, a center fountain, a children's playground, and a 3D walk-in house)
- Stratum Oil Industries (the company's second office location)
- Valora Docks (a docking port for fisherman with two warehouses for housing boats)
- First National Bank

- Valousse Convention Center
- SpeedWay Rail Stations (SpeedWay Rail Trains going in and out of the city)
- TechStrumm Industries

Laroouse City, Illinois (an hour and thirty minutes west of Valousse City, IL)

- Skyyas Airport

Methphodollous Island (located somewhere close off the East Coast of the United States)

- Primous Facility (a facility that houses psychotic individuals who have had mental breakdowns, hardened criminals, and the like; there is also talk of the facility being used to hold cross-humans)

Naphilia Town, Illinois (forty minutes east of Hidendale Springs, IL)

- SpeedWay Rail Lines (SpeedWay Rail Train going in and out of the town)
- Sysis June Lake (the beach on which DiLuAH's ship crashed-landed at night)
- A HighTech City soldier was instructed to go to Naphilia Town

Ococo Town, Illinois (west of Tarainound Street, leaving Hidendale Springs, IL)

- VeVideer Forest (a huge forest twenty miles from Hidendale Springs, IL)

This place is of little importance right now …

Gyrasion Providence, Illinois (two hours and thirty minutes west of Tarainound Street)

- A seaport allowing US Navy ships to dock because a base is located in the area

Lamont Town, Michigan (one hour and forty minutes north of Hidendale Springs, IL)

- Teekee Forest (a huge forest)

College Station, Texas (A city in East Central Texas in the heart of the Brazos Valley)

- SpeedWay Rail Stations (a station where multiple trains leave and enter from different cities and states around the world and the station that connects to Melova-Metro Train Station in Melovaton City, South Carolina)
- Stratum Oil Industries (main office location)
- Stratum Oil Employees Parking Garage (located outside of Stratum Oil Industry's main office building)

Port Aransas, Texas (A city in Nueces County, TX)

- Stratum Oil Industries (Fourth location)
- Shipyard (Dozens of boats are stored. One warehouse that is always deserted.)

Arnesto Capital, Texas (an island on the southern Texas border, which points to Baton Rouge, LA)

Varilin Capitol, New York (A new, small island city sixty minutes from New York City)

- Home of Sam Kerry's family

In the year 2020, California broke into three new peninsulas, which drifted from California's original position. **Oirailie Island** is a new island that drifted north and is now the Northern California Peninsula. Oirailie Island's eastern beach points toward Washington State. **Sandulay Island** is the second newest island, which drifted west and is far off on its own. **Qudruewley Island** is the third newest island. It drifted southeast. The three new California peninsulas, all large islands, each have a Northern Beach, an Eastern Beach, a Southern Beach, and a Western Beach.

New Waii Island is a small island located somewhere in the Atlantic Ocean. At the end of the twenty-first century (2095) an island lifted from under water in the middle of the Atlantic Ocean, right across somewhere near the south part of South America. A few people from all over the world flocked to and inhabited this new island. The island became overpopulated within a few short months. The island is believed to be the lost city of Atlantis that disappeared a long time ago. A few nonbelievers that say this is a fairy tale. The people of the new island are referred to as, Atlantis Dwellers. Within a year, a city was built. Still the only city on the island, it is called **New Waii City**.

Basement (an unknown location where Scientist Mario Vega does his secret experiments and invents new technology. Mario Vega never sees the light of day.)

Appendix 2

The V-Link is a high-tech digital watch that combines with the user's central nervous system. It transforms the civilian into his or her agent gear, is use to summon artillery and weapons, can teleport the agent, and is activated by the agent's thoughts and physical movements. Its features include:

- **headset**. The V-Link headset is worn on the forehead and used to communicate with people who are also wearing one
- **V-Cuffs**. A small, round, slick piece of metal that opens into a spiral and binds around an enemy to immobilize the person.
- **Invisi-Dome**. A circular barrier used to cover an area of a city or town, which cannot be seen by normal civilians and also prevents them from seeing what is happening inside the barrier – Invisi-Domes keep civilians safe and prevent foes from escaping. Any VLORs member with a V-Link can enter a dome. Once activated, a dome affects all technology in the area, and any normal civilian inside one will have his or her memory of the experience automatically erased. Invisi-Domes also have restoring properties to fix property damage.
- **tiny grenade pellets**. Exploding bombs that don't do heavy damage
- **flame igniter**. Resembles a pocket lighter, but thin and long. Produces quick flame.
- **deflector shield**. A near invisible shield. Once activated, it's in the shape of a circle. You'll be able to see through it but nothing can get through.
- **gasoline capsules**. A capsule that contains gasoline inside it.
- **holo-messages**. 3D telephone calls.
- **Q3 explosives**. Small devices that send sonic screeches to clear away particles such as dirt, small rocks, and the like.
- **Q6 explosives**. Medium-sized devices that sends sonic screeches to clear away heavier material.

- **Q9 explosives**. Small, cubed devices that expand and send sonic screeches that can destroy everything within a one-mile radius.
- **scope lens**. A tool that gives the agent the ability to see through walls.
- **tiny daggers**. Tiny swords for throwing at your opponent, used only by Agent Rahz.
- **Tracker.** A small disk, about the size of an American dime that, when attached to anything, allows the user to follow an individual.
- **BIO-Beings.** A new technology not revealed until book 2, manufactured using Anaheim's technology. Digital human bodies made to engage in missions as part of a project that was terminated after CURDUR (an evil inside Agent Z) was born.
- **V-Inducer.** A small object that, when thrown, closes around an object or a physical being. Once trapped, whatever is inside the V-Inducer is destroyed by a blaze of fire. Nothing can resist the intense flames a V-Inducer can produce.

Appendix 3

New technology created by scientist Rayley Nickolson:

- **Vactra boots**. Footwear with built-in gliding and rocket devices that enables agents to go airborne or to skate two inches off the ground.
- **Vactra flight board**. A glider that materializes from Z's V-Link and Agent Z's mode of transport.
- **Vactra sword**. Agent Z learns to become a master swordsman. The Vactra sword was his first sword.
- **Vactra cutters**. Lower left and right arm blades that eject from devices on the agent's wrists and Caj's main weapon.
- **Vactra daggers**. Sharp twin blades and Rahz's main weapon.
- **Vactra blasters**. A blaster that every agent is equipped with, which emits a laser that can be shot at enemies.
- **Vactra armor**. Only one agent who will utilize. An arm extender with blaster. It starts out as a metallic band then it'll expand, making a full arm blaster. Eventually, with updates, it'll be a full-body suit of armor.
- **Vactra bubbles**. Transparent bubble traps.
- **Vactra boppers**. Boxing gloves that pack a devastating, dynamic punch.
- **Vactra cycle**. Operated only by Rev, who travels from the islands to the States to help other agents.

New technology that originated from an unknown and now disbanded clan, once located in the country of Japan:

- **Shibarion blade**. A redesigned sword that becomes Agent Z's main weapon.
- **Shibarion blade-blaster**. This change shape and transform from a blaster into a sword.
- **Shibarion swigger**. A redesigned weapon that can change shape, a transformer between a tracer and a whip. This to be just a whip.

Appendix 4

Mysterious Miscellaneous Objects

- **repliara crystatite**. A rare crystal that copies a person's identity. If the imposter's appearance cracks, white lights expel out of the person who has taken another's appearance, returning that person to his or her normal self.
- **The flamethrower unit**. Invented by scientist Curtis Anaheim, the fire starter. It resembles a normal MK-47, only larger.
- **SupeXoil**. Capsules containing a viscous liquid derived from petroleum that can be used as a fuel or lubricant. The petroleum has been modified with an unknown substance. The scientist created this technology is a mystery. This special oil was converted from crude oil to diesel fuel and then to an unknown chemical. It is used to power machines and only Stratum Oil Industries has access to it.
- **SupeXelectric**. Capsules containing an electric substance used to power machines and created by Stratum Oil Industries.
- **Dale's QPad**. A money transfer device used by Dale Jr. It is just an electronic keypad.

Appendix 5

VLORs & VICE: Timeline

1999

- Krarnaca crash-landed on Earth.

2007

- This year marked the end of the Shoc'Weillers and the Jolt'Tweillers, a race of lightning warriors and a superior form of homosapiens. A secret government assault was ordered by the president of the United States on December 31, 2007. This mysterious race of people had to be extinguished because they were a danger to mankind, according to the U.S. Military.
- Guardian Gai was attacked. Struck with an illness, he died on October 1, 2007. Tundarick was also killed that same day.

2020

- California broke into three new peninsulas, which drifted from California's original position. **Oirailie Island** is a new island that drifted north and becomes the Northern California Peninsula. Oirailie Island's eastern beach points toward the state of Washington. **Sandulay Island** is a new island that drifted west, and is far off on its own. This is the Western California Peninsula. **Qudruewley Island** drifted southeast and becomes the Southern California Peninsula. The three new California peninsulas all have a Northern Beach, an Eastern Beach, a Southern Beach, and a Western Beach. All three peninsulas are huge and contain many cities.

2030

- This year saw a marked rise in unemployment in the United States.
- Dale Falakar Sr. had four Stratum Oil facilities built in various places in the United States.

2068

- Madin Doro Torres was born.

2076

- Xavier Marshall was born

2079

- Tundarick was reborn.

2080

- A mysterious sheet of metal crashed on planet Earth. Naralina was born.

2082

- Samuel Marshall brought his six year old son Xavier to a secret lab on Northern Beach in Oirailie Island. The secret lab was destroyed.

2085

- DiLuAH's ship recovered from its malfunction in outer space, and his ship crashed on planet Earth near Sysis June Lake in Naphilia Town, IL. The ship exploded, and the passenger escaped. Miles away in Hidendale Springs, IL, where he had long been buried in a cave deep underneath the city, the cursed knight's tomb cracked open.

2088

- Xavier Marshall returned home with father after a long trip.

2089

- Xavier Marshall fell in love with beautiful girl. Drey was born. Michel Johnson was born.

2090

- Jack McKoy was born. Ronald Osaida was born. Krarnaca, now known as Doc Krarn, was hired into VICE.
- In June of this year, unemployment dropped 10 percent in the United States.

2091

- Jodana Uvarla was born.

2092

- Jacque Baller was born. Joel Rodriquez was born. Lin Yiu Gustov was born. Gai Tunh Chi was reborn.

2093

- Xavier Marshall collapsed and has been in a coma ever since. Rhin Kashioko was born. Jennifer Wayner was born.

2094

- Zadarion 'Z' Jones was born. Zhariah 'Rahz' Johnson was born. Jayla Price was born. Kiyla Gerald was born. Alecxander 'Shocker' Jackson was born.

2095

- A new island floated up somewhere in the Atlantic Ocean and was officially named New Waii Island. Rivi was born and later found on the island by Krojo. Valery Maxill was born.

2096

- Eraine 'Floral' Delpro've was born.

2097

- Mayana's parents arrived on Earth.

2098

- A young knight (Jaylin) was born. The mysterious cursed knight crawled out from under Drenden Mountain, located in Hidendale Springs, IL. The cursed knight explored the new world.

2100

- Mayana 'Maya' Johnson was born.

2103

- Joel Rodriguez became a cross-human. He started calling himself, ShaVenger.

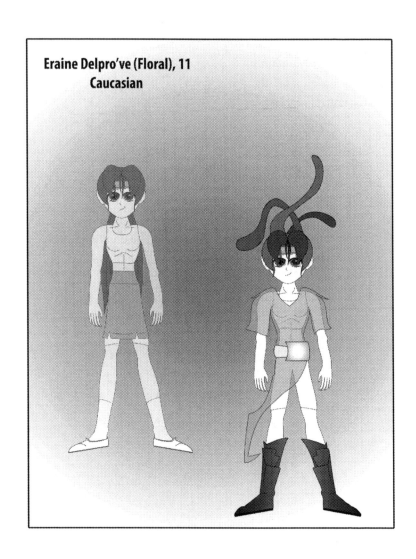

Eraine Delpro've (Floral), 11
Caucasian

Agent Caj (Jack McKoy), 17
Caucasian

Joel Rodriguez (ShaVenger), 15
Cuban and African American

Ryan Zada Jones, 13
Black, White & Indian

Mhariah Zari Johnson, 13
Black, White & Indian

Alecxander Jackson (Shocker), 13 and 8
Shoc'Weiller & Jolt'Tweiller

Tim McGraw, 62
Caucasian American

Alexander Torres, 28
Caucasian American

Lisa Miller, 35
African American

Angela Runn, 18
Caucasian American

Dani and Rani Darivele, 13
Caucasian Americans

Dave and Hailie Jones,33
White / Black and African American

Grandpa Jedediah Jones, 68
Native American

David Mikaelson, 16
Australian

Richard Davis Bloome, 16
Caucasian

Samuel Kerry, 13
African American

Mitchel Conald, 16
African American

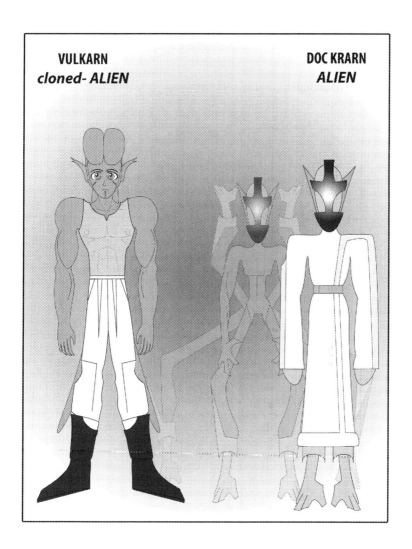

VULKARN
cloned- ALIEN

DOC KRARN
ALIEN

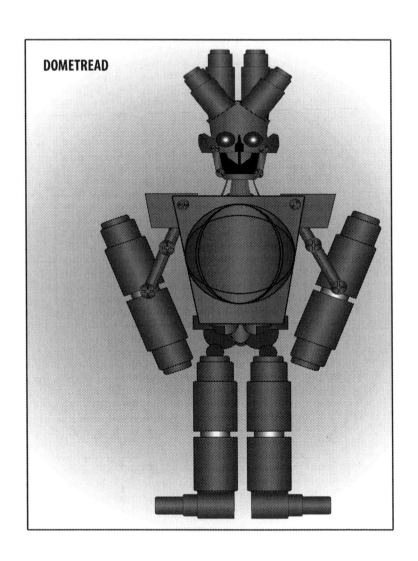

DOMETREAD

Darryl 'Domos' Langford, 27
Somalian and African American

Ray 'Snake' Gardner, 32
Race Unknown

Cloudis Monroe, 52
Native American

Ronald Battleton, 36
Caucasian

Tundarick (Derick Jackson), 28
Shoc'Weiller

Gai Tunh Chi, 15
Guardian

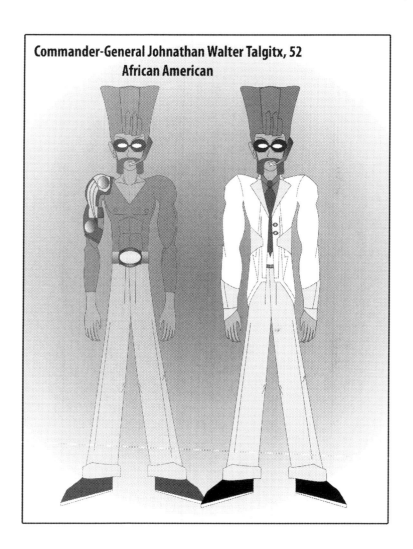

Commander-General Johnathan Walter Talgitx, 52
African American

Mrs. Janet Mulon, 68   Cameron Casey, 38
Caucasian American   Irish American

Andrew 'Techy Andy' Mathessen, 24
Caucasian American

Michel Johnson, 18
Caucasian American

Jayla Price, 13
African American

Morgan Wiles, 13
Caucasian American

Kiyla Gerald, 13
Dominican

Maya Johnson, 7
Caucasian American

KYROS-X TEAM
An evil crime syndicate

Cloudis, Domos, Ron and Snake

Lilori 'Prof. Dila' Daniels, 28
Caucasian

DILUSION

DiLuAH
Alien

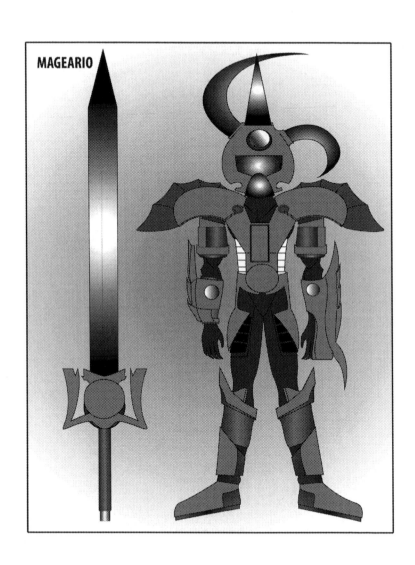

MAGEARIO

Pesto've 'Pyro' Daggerton, 38
Caucasian

Dale Falakar Jr., 58
African American

Darius 'Dyro' Helms, 29
Caucasian

Max Gerald, 22
Caucasian

STATISTABOTS

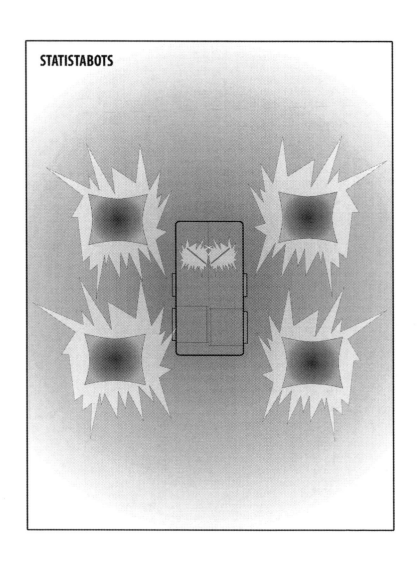

Co. Thomas Jeffery Addams, 32
Caucasian American

Matthew Delpro've, 36
Caucasian American

Nick, 42
Black

Mario Vega, 39
Mexican

Pedro, 48
Spanish

Ted, 35
Caucasian

This box is the Global Locator. You can view all kinds of activity using this tool. It allows to zoom in and out, travel distances, environmental and situational awareness, etc.

This box accesses your headset. Speak with any member of your team using this tool.

This box accesses your arsenal. Like a computer, a separate tab appears and a list of all available weapons, gadgets, etc. are available for your choosing.

This is a marking of specific locations.

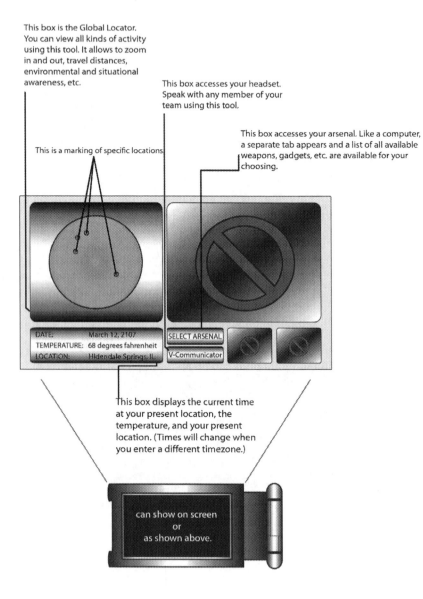

DATE: March 12, 2107
TEMPERATURE: 68 degrees fahrenheit
LOCATION: Hidendale Springs, IL

SELECT ARSENAL

V-Communicator

This box displays the current time at your present location, the temperature, and your present location. (Times will change when you enter a different timezone.)

can show on screen
or
as shown above.

what's coming in...

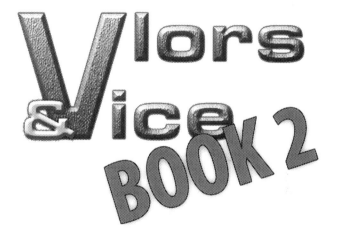

BIO - GENETIC ORGANISM

10124211125222100   10124211125222100
10024216425224802   10024216425224802
10874216425264110   10874216425264110
10564000024500212   10564000024500212

BIO-Beings ——

A new technology manufactured using Anaheim's technology. Digital human bodies made to engage in missions as part of a project that was terminated after an evil was born.

About the Author

Sean L Johnson, currently working in the United States Navy, has an Associates in Arts (A.A.) degree from Prairie State College. I am a new author, wanting to finally express my otherworldly thoughts. I enjoy watching anime, even to this day. Anime, as well as many movies, inspire me to see new things. There are wonderful things hidden in the smallest places. I enjoy hand drawing cartoon characters, painting displaying realism and doing photography. Currently, I am working on bettering myself.

Printed in the United States
By Bookmasters